LOOK BACK ON MURDER

Thirty years ago The White House, now owned by television personality Miles Jordan, was the scene of a murder. The owner Nigel Randall was found shot in the summerhouse, his wife Susan was convicted of the murder and died in prison. Private Detective Alan Craig was invited by Jordan to a Country House Weekend. When he meets his fellow guests he learns that some of them were present when Randall had been murdered. Clearly Jordan is up to something. But what? Before Craig can find out there is another murder in the summerhouse.

MALCOLM GRAY

LOOK BACK ON MURDER

Complete and Unabridged

LINFORD
Leicester

First published in Great Britain in 1985 by
Ross Anderson Publications Ltd.,
Bolton

First Linford Mystery Edition
published January 1989

British Library CIP Data

Gray, Malcolm, *1927*–
    Look back on murder.—Large print ed.—
Linford mystery library
    Rn: Ian Stuart   I. Title
823′.914[F]

ISBN 0-7089-6630-6

Published by
F. A. Thorpe (Publishing) Ltd.
Anstey, Leicestershire
Set by Rowland Phototypesetting Ltd.
Bury St. Edmunds, Suffolk
Printed and bound in Great Britain by
T. J. Press (Padstow) Ltd., Padstow, Cornwall

Prologue

LORRAINE MAXWELL sighed. Back home in Hollywood coming to England had seemed like a good idea. After all, she hadn't been back for years, and then only for a few days. Now she was here she was no longer so sure.

I'm tired, she thought. That's all it is. Everything will be different tomorrow.

Nobody could be expected to be at their best after flying nearly 6,000 miles in a roaring, overheated jet, and she hadn't been able to sleep because every time she closed her eyes that tedious woman in the green pants suit had started talking again. Then there were the photographers' lights in her face at Heathrow and the reporters bombarding her with questions. When all she wanted was to get to her hotel and sleep.

Face it, honey, she told herself, ten years ago

you'd have loved it. You'd have bandied words with the reporters and scored a few points and everybody would have had a ball. The trouble is you're not so young any more. Okay, so she was fit and stuffed with vitamin pills and heaven knew what else, but her fifty-third birthday loomed depressingly near.

"There's some mail, Lorrie," her secretary said.

"Let it wait." Lorraine sat down at the dressing-table and picked up a hair brush.

"Most of it's routine, I guess," Barbara Foster told her, glancing at the letters. "There's an invitation to spend a weekend from some guy called Miles Jordan."

"From Miles?"

"You know him?"

"We met at a party in New York, and I had lunch with him once. He has one of the top TV shows over here."

"Oh him." Barbara dismissed Miles Jordan; people were always asking Lorrie to lunch or dinner. "The party's at some place called The White House, Lower Marking. Say, I didn't know there was a White House in England." Barbara laughed.

Lorraine's hand had stopped in mid-air, still

holding the brush. "Did you say Lower Marking?" she demanded.

"That's right. Why, have you been there?"

"I went once, a long time ago. It's a village about forty miles outside of London. I used to know some people who lived there."

She had been staying with them that terrible day when . . . It had taken her a long time to put behind her what happened then and the consequences, but eventually she had succeeded. Now here was this invitation bringing it all back.

It couldn't be the same house. Lower Marking was the sort of village where smart and successful people like Miles Jordan often chose to live, picturesque and not too far from London. There were probably at least a dozen other houses they had taken over. Anyway, that other house had been called something different. But it had been white, standing graceful and strangely ethereal when seen from a distance at the crest of the gentle slope up from the river.

Lorraine shook herself mentally. It was absurd even thinking they could be the same, she was allowing the effects of the flight to make her fanciful. If only there hadn't been something in Miles' face which struck a chord in her memory. Something she couldn't identify.

"Do you want I should make the usual polite excuse?" Barbara enquired.

Lorraine didn't answer at once. Then she said over her shoulder, "No, I think I'll go. I'll write myself tomorrow." Her features stared back at her from the mirror, pale, almost gaunt.

"Okay."

Lorrie looked real pooped, Barbara thought. She'd never seen her quite this way before. Oh well, everybody knew long flights could play funny tricks with your system. She didn't feel that hot herself. A couple of days and Lorrie would be back to her normal self, the glamorous, confident star.

It was only later she remembered that Lorraine hadn't looked shocked in quite that way until she told her about the invitation.

"That chap Miles Jordan wants us to go down to his place for a weekend," Charles Laxton said, helping himself to marmalade. "D'you want to go?"

His wife lowered the letter she had been reading and regarded him over the top of her half-glasses. The letter was from the chairman of the local Conservative Women's Association and irritating; Helen Rochford only wrote when she believed she had cause for complaint about something or, more often, somebody. "I wonder what he wants," she said.

"Wants?" Laxton queried.

"You don't think he would invite us if he didn't want something, do you? There's always an ulterior motive with people like that."

"In television, you mean?" Laxton had great respect for his wife's powers of perception but now, as she often did, she was confusing him.

"We hardly know him, why should he ask us if he doesn't want something?" Elizabeth went on, ignoring the question. "It can hardly be that he agrees with your views. He's brash and pushing. But what can you expect, he has no breeding." She sighed. "Still, I suppose we had better go."

Laxton grunted. At 61 he had something of the appearance of an emaciated eagle with high, rather prominent cheekbones and a thin beak of a nose. But if age had withered him, it hadn't mellowed his opinions; he had been on the right of the Party when he entered Parliament twenty-odd years ago and, although it had moved to the right itself since then, he still was. He was not an unkind man and, whatever they thought of his attitudes, most of his fellow-members quite liked him, but he was incapable of understanding anybody else's point of view. He might pontificate, but outside a small minority nobody paid much attention.

Yet thirty years ago he had seemed to have a future. He had gone into the Army straight from school, and come out of it again in 1946 at the age of 23, a captain in an infantry regiment with an MC and no qualifications for civilian life. Through a friend's introduction he had joined a large firm of estate agents in the West End, people liked him, and by the time he was 30 he seemed set on the road which would lead in due course to a partnership and a pleasant house in the outer suburbs. It was then that he was persuaded to go into politics, and life was never the same again.

It seemed to him now it had all started with that beastly business at the Randalls'. They had lived at Lower Marking too. Odd that.

"He's probably after support for some scheme he's hatching," Elizabeth remarked. "Or he's looking for a public figure to sit on the board of one of his companies."

"I hadn't thought of that," Laxton said, brightening. He was proud of being an MP. He loved the ritual and the fellowship, being part of a great tradition, and, despite the behaviour of some of the newer Members and their open contempt for the things he believed in, he still saw Parliament as the tabernacle of Britain's greatness. When people showed respect for his being a Member of it he was gratified.

"Yes," Elizabeth said, "I think we should go." Those dreadful people! she thought with distaste.

Laxton's optimism was short-lived. Soon he remembered the public figures Jordan had crucified on his programme and he began to feel distinctly uneasy. Was it possible Jordan had found out about Hepton's retainer?

The more he thought about it the more worried he became.

"We're not going," Simon Fenn said, his voice rising.

Gabriella stared at him, a dangerous glint in her magnificent eyes and her full lips pouting.

"You may not go," she told him, "but I will." Although her father was Italian-born, Gabriella had first seen the light of day in

Wembley, and she had been to Italy only twice in her life. Nevertheless she had discovered at an early age that there were times when an assumed Italian accent could be an advantage to a girl. She had adopted it so often that now it was second nature to her.

Fenn eyed her suspiciously. "You told me it was all over between you and Jordan," he said.

"Per'aps I was wrong. 'E loved me so much and now 'e 'as found 'e cannot live without me." Gabriella paused. "Why do you think he asked you to write the scripts for those programmes? 'E 'ad never read your books, 'e told me so. It was because of me."

She was motivated by malice, Fenn knew that, but was what she said true? He had never done any work for television before Jordan asked him. It had been a breakthrough and he had prided himself that his talents were being rewarded at last. The idea that he might have been asked only as a return for his wife's favours wounded and angered him. There were times when he could cheerfully have strangled Gabriella.

"Let's go, Simon. Please." Her tone had changed, she was pleading now, and the expression in her eyes had softened. "Then I can let him see that for me it is all over and it is you I love. Can't we, darling?"

"All right," Fenn agreed bitterly. He was by no means convinced that he was doing the right thing, indeed he had an uneasy feeling that if they went it could well be disastrous, but when Gabriella asked him like that his resolution evaporated. He knew that he was spineless and that she would probably betray him as she had done so often in the past, but somehow it made no difference.

He told himself it wasn't her fault; she couldn't help being susceptible. Jordan had started it all, it was Jordan he should be thinking of killing.

1

IN view of everything that happened afterwards it would have been fitting if the letter had landed on Craig's mat with a dramatic thud. Instead it wafted through the letter-box to alight gently a yard from the door.

Georgie found it there when she brought Craig his coffee. Georgie, who was 19 years old, dark and pertly pretty, acted as receptionist and general clerk for the electrical contractors across the landing from whom Craig rented his two rooms. The day after he moved in she saw him crossing the landing about 10.30 and asked if he would like a cup of coffee. He said, thanks very much, he would, and since then she had brought him coffee in the mornings and tea in the afternoons five days a week when he was in. It was no hardship for her, she was a normal, warm hearted girl, and Craig at 34 was five feet eleven and well built, with brown hair, grey eyes and lean features.

When Georgie came in this morning he was

lying back in his chair reading an old number of *Private Eye.*

"Where d'you get that?" she enquired.

Craig lowered the magazine enough to regard her over the top of it. "You may not know," he informed her in a superior tone he intended to be crushing, "but this is the inquiry agent's professional journal."

"Garn!" Georgie grinned engagingly. "Where d'yer get it?"

Craig sighed. "If you must know, my dentist's waiting room. I've had two damned great fillings this morning." He paused defensively. "Well, he didn't want it, and he owed me more than that for what he put me through. Anyway, I subscribe to the National Health, don't I? It was partly mine."

"You just want to read what it says about people," Georgie said cheerfully.

"In this job you have to know what's going on."

"Was going on, you mean. It's two months old."

"And be in the swim," Craig continued, sweeping the interruption aside as if by a powerful breast stroke. "Clients expect it."

Her innate kindness prevented Georgie

2

asking what clients. "There's a letter for you," she said, putting down Craig's coffee and handing him the envelope.

During the three weeks since Alan Craig Associates had commenced business—there were no Associates, Craig had invented them to impress potential clients (apparently without success, clients were noticeable only by their absence)—thirteen envelopes had dropped through his letter-box. Eight had contained bills and three circulars. That, he reckoned, made the odds on this one also demanding payment for something about two to one. It was a depressing prospect.

Not that it looked like a bill. The envelope was large and the paper of good quality, stiff, white and slightly rough in texture. On the other hand, it didn't look like an offer of work either. The only jobs Alan Craig Associates had had in its brief existence had come from a bank (Craig's own, which therefore had a vested interest in his survival) and a firm of country solicitors. How they had obtained his name he couldn't imagine. Neither had wasted money on expensive stationery.

When the door had closed behind Georgie he slit the envelope and from it extracted two photostat sheets stapled together at one corner. There was no covering letter, not even as much as a compliment slip to show who had sent them, and the postmark was London W. Which told you damn all, he thought, unfolding the sheets.

They were a copy of a newspaper report. That the paper had been old was obvious for the photostats showed signs of its discoloration and the marks of splitting and curling along the edges. In the margin somebody had printed in block letters "HERALD & CHRONICLE 11 NOV 1954".

A headline, "PLAYBOY'S WIFE TO HANG. SUSAN RANDALL GUILTY", extended across most of the page, and under it was a long and fairly detailed report of a trial. Clearly the case had been something of a *cause célèbre* at the time. Locally, at least. As far as he could remember Craig had never heard of it.

He studied the photograph of the condemned woman. It was blurred and indistinct, but even so there was no doubt Susan Randall had been a beauty. Her oval face was framed by dark hair and, although her lips were smiling, there was a haunting sadness about her eyes. The smile might be misleading, Craig thought, assumed for the photographer's benefit, but the face didn't look like that of a passionate woman. Still, who could tell?

He wondered if she had appealed successfully. If not, almost certainly she had been reprieved. Very few women had been executed in Britain since the war and he was pretty sure Susan Randall hadn't been among them. She would be fifty-eight or fifty-nine now, if she was still alive.

He studied the envelope curiously. Why hadn't whoever sent it enclosed some explanation? Or, at least, some clue to his or her identity?

He put it down again and started reading the story which occupied most of the two pages. Susan Randall and her husband Nigel had been popular members of what prosecuting counsel called—Craig could imagine his assumed distaste—"a somewhat fast set". Which probably meant that they gave rather noisy parties for their London friends, they drove fast cars, the women dressed smartly, and they had little to do with their neighbours.

Randall was a financier, whatever that meant; it was the sort of emotive description journalists loved. He had bought Bensons, a largish house on the outskirts of the village of Lower Marking, a year before the murder and lived there with his wife and their only child, staying in a flat in Town during the week and driving down on Friday evenings.

On the July weekend when he died there were eight guests at Bensons. One of them, a Mrs. Caroline Bateman, had testified that about three o'clock on the Saturday afternoon she had strolled down to the stream which flowed past the south side of the grounds. Walking back to rejoin her husband, who had been playing tennis with some of the other guests, she had met him on a path which led through the wood separating the gardens from the river bank. They had walked on together and almost immediately had met Susan Randall who asked them if they had seen her husband. Mrs. Bateman told her that she had heard somebody in the summerhouse on the bank as she passed and she hurried on in that direction. A minute or two later the Batemans had heard a shot and, running to the summerhouse, had found Mrs. Randall there standing beside her husband's body, a revolver on the ground by her feet. He had been shot through the right temple at close range. Not close enough, however, according to the pathologist, for him to have fired the shot himself. There were no finger-prints on the gun and Mrs. Randall was wearing thin white gloves. That had counted against her. Even in the Fifties, it seemed, young women didn't wear gloves on hot summer days unless they were going out.

The prosecution established that she and her husband had quarrelled frequently. She didn't deny it, her defence was that she had gone to tell him that she had to go into the village and to ask him to return to their guests. He was dead when she reached the summerhouse. But neither of the Batemans had seen anybody else in the wood, and Mrs. Bateman agreed reluctantly that Mrs. Randall had seemed distraught when they met her. The accused woman herself didn't claim to have seen anyone.

It was common knowledge that Randall had had affairs with a succession of women, but none of the guests appeared to have any motive for killing him and the verdict was almost a foregone conclusion. The jury was out for less than two hours.

Craig picked up his cup and drank the rest of his coffee. It was cold.

To judge from the report, it had been an

open and shut case. Moreover it had happened nearly thirty years ago and to all intents and purposes it was forgotten. Who had taken the trouble to copy the old report and send it to him after all this time? Just as intriguing, why?

Craig picked up his phone and dialled an old colleague's number. They talked for a few minutes and when he put the phone down again he knew one thing at least: whoever had sent him the report it hadn't been Susan Randall. She had died in prison in 1961.

The next morning's post brought a request from another branch of his bank to trace a customer named Hollins who had run up an overdraft of over £600 by fraudulent use of his cheque card, then disappeared, and an envelope, smaller and square but otherwise identical with that which had contained the photostats.

This one held only a card on which was printed:

Miles Jordan
requests the pleasure of your company
at a weekend party
at
The White House, Lower Marking
Dinner, Friday 15 July RSVP

Craig stared at it in disbelief. The only Miles Jordan of whom he had heard was the jet-setting television star whose face was as familiar to most people in Britain as that of the Prime Minister. His programme, transmitted at a peak viewing time every week for several months of the year, had become almost a part of life for half the adult population. More people were said to watch it than any other non-fiction programme on any channel.

It was investigative journalism shown live, but, also, something more than that. There had been accusatory series on television before, plenty of them, but none with the daring and flair of *The Miles Jordan Hour*. Sometimes it dealt with unsolved mysteries, sometimes with swindles perpetrated on unwitting victims by powerful groups, or injustices by government departments, but always the subject of a programme was kept secret until the very last minute. On the one occasion when a newspaper had discovered the theme, that programme was scrapped and another substituted for it.

Jordan stood for no mealy mouthed nonsense about not naming the people he saw as guilty, and half the production team had been threatened with legal action at least once. So far none of the threats had been carried out, and there were critics who claimed that Jordan chose his targets carefully, selecting only people who, for one reason or another, couldn't retaliate. Those critics accused the programme of appealing to the basest instincts of their audiences, to a primitive, sadistic delight in seeing prominent people humiliated and destroyed. Jordan claimed that he was never sued because his victims were always guilty and dared not risk taking him to court.

The public didn't care either way, and the shows were presented with a lavish brilliance which made other producers green with envy. They had also made Jordan famous.

Craig read the invitation a second time. He couldn't believe Miles Jordan was inviting him, a perfect stranger, to his house for a weekend party. Why should he? Then he saw that the card didn't invite him personally, it simply requested "your" company. That explained it, some secretary must have slipped it into the wrong envelope. Or got the wrong Alan Craig.

And yet . . . The envelope matched the one which had come yesterday, and that had been addressed to Alan Craig Associates. Also, Jordan's house was in the same village as

Bensons where Susan Randall had murdered her husband. Was that only coincidence?

It was conceivable that Jordan might be interested in a thirty year old murder case if he saw a way in which he could use it as a peg for a programme, like a miscarriage of justice—not that that seemed likely here—but why send the report to him? And why invite him to his party? Craig had two or three acquaintances who worked in television, but none of them possessed the influence to pull that sort of invitation, even if he had asked them to.

And if they had, it still wouldn't explain the first envelope. None of it made sense.

He told himself he wouldn't go. Jordan and his friends inhabited a different world, one where he would feel out of place and uncomfortable.

"Miles Jordan's invited me for a weekend," he told Georgie when she brought his coffee.

"Garn."

"It's true." Craig showed her the card.

"Are you going?"

"No. It's not my scene."

Georgie gave the card a second look. "Why should 'e ask you? I mean . . ."

Craig grinned. "I expect he wants somebody to keep an eye on the silver."

"You go. If you don't you'll wish afterwards you 'ad. Think 'oo may be there." Georgie's eyes became dreamy with the thought. "Besides, you'll always wonder why 'e asked you. Maybe 'e's like the Queen an' asks all sorts of diff'rent people to mix 'em up like."

Craig laughed. But he knew that she was right and that if he didn't go he would wonder. And although he might protest, already he had almost decided to accept the invitation—if only because he was curious. Not merely about the reason for Jordan's inviting him, but about the old report too.

"I'll see," he said. "When I've had my coffee I'm going out, Georgie. I'll switch the machine on, but if anybody comes, I'll be back some time this afternoon."

"Okay," Georgie agreed cheerfully.

Craig spent most of the remainder of that day trying to trace the elusive Hollins. The trail led him from Mortlake to Hammersmith, out to Croydon, then east to Lewisham. He met indignant landladies and angry tradesmen, but in the end all he learnt was that Cliff Hollins was a plausible rogue who had lived pretty well at other people's expense for three or four months and, just possibly, had moved on to Brighton.

By the time he got back to his office it was past six. There were no messages from Georgie and he switched on his answering machine.

"This is Waltex Equipment," a voice said coldly, its tones slightly distorted by the machine. "We have received no reply to our letters of the 12 May and 14 June and we have to inform you that if our account isn't settled within the next fourteen days we shall institute legal proceedings."

"Get knotted," Craig said bitterly.

The machine was talking again. "Good afternoon, Mr. Craig. This is Judith Cromer, Miles Jordan's personal assistant." There was nothing cold about Miss Cromer's voice, it was low-pitched and succeeded in being businesslike and intriguing at the same time. "Mr. Jordan would like to call to see you at 11.30 tomorrow morning, Mr. Craig. He hopes that will suit you, but if it isn't convenient, perhaps you would be kind enough to ring me and we can arrange another time." There followed a telephone number, then Miss Cromer said goodbye.

There were no more messages and Craig sat

staring at the machine. Why did Jordan want to come to see him? It couldn't be merely to explain that the invitation had been sent to him by mistake and apologise, a phone call would have sufficed for that. A job? If a man in Jordan's position was coming to him instead of one of the old established firms he must have a good reason—and that suggested it was either (a) something he wanted as few people as possible to know about or (b) the big firms wouldn't take it on.

Craig picked up the phone and dialled a Brighton number. The man he wanted to speak to had gone home, so he left a message for him to ring back and made a note in his diary to check in the morning whether he could send Waltex Equipment a cheque without the near certainty that it would bounce. Under it he made another: "11.30 Miles Jordan." Then he locked up and went home to his flat in Belsize Park.

There was no post the next morning. Craig checked his cash book, decided he could pay Waltex and made out a cheque. Doing so gave him a good feeling, as if he had scored a point off an enemy.

Miles Jordan arrived promptly at 11.30. He was about Craig's age but shorter and slimmer than he looked on television, with dark wavy hair and intelligent dark eyes. He was wearing a modishly informal suit and an open necked shirt, and there was about him a suggestion of restless energy which was only partly concealed by his relaxed manner. Although his face was familiar, it seemed to Craig that it was different in some way from the picture he had seen so often, as if the television cameras obliterated its subtleties. Yet it seemed to him that it was a public face, a mask behind which the real man hid. He told himself he was being fanciful, imagining things because Jordan was who he was.

"Hallo, Alan." Jordan smiled and held out his hand.

Craig was used to people who called him by his Christian name within a couple of minutes of their first meeting. They always made him withdraw a little.

"Come in, Mr. Jordan," he said.

Jordan walked through into the inner office and sat down, looking round him. "You don't remember me," he said. "Oh well, it's a long time."

Craig sat in his chair behind the desk and tried to remember where he had met the other man before. "A long time?" he repeated.

Jordan laughed. Something in that laugh, a barely discernible note of triumph, told Craig his visitor had intended him to be surprised, had even introduced this theatrical touch deliberately, and was pleased he had reacted according to plan. The knowledge irritated him.

"Think back," Jordan said. "Lancaster Grove Comprehensive."

Craig stretched his memory. It was nearly twenty years ago, but he remembered the shabby corridors with their stone floors and discoloured paint and the vaguely depressing classrooms vividly. Only Miles Jordan eluded him.

"I was Michael then," Jordan told him.

Michael? No, Micky. Of course. Craig remembered now. Micky Jordan, the bright boy at the end of the row, good-looking and self-confident even then. Not with the loud, empty bravado of some of the others but with a sort of inner assurance. Sophisticated even at sixteen. He had mixed easily and been accepted by the roughest of his fellows, partly because of his natural charm and partly because of an impish streak which surfaced at times, leading him into pranks and saving him from accusations of priggishness. Yet he had seemed in some way apart from them. A loner. And if the inevitable abbreviation of his Christian name had seemed inappropriate then, it seemed doubly so now.

"Micky!" Craig exclaimed.

Jordan's smile widened. "You got my invitation?"

"Yes. Why me? What's it all about?"

"Does it have to be about anything?" Jordan inquired innocently. "I'm giving a party and I'd like you to come."

"You expect me to believe that? After nearly twenty years?"

"Partly because of that. It's time."

"I've got a suspicious nature," Craig said.

"Ah yes, all those years in the police."

"That's right."

"Why did you leave, Alan?"

"Personal reasons."

"It's all right, I know why," Jordan told him.

Craig stared at the other man. You bastard, he thought. That's why you've traced me after all this time, you want to use me, to take what happened and make something out of it for your programme.

"That's how you found me," he said.

"Right. We're doing a feature, I talked to a few people, and your name came up. I made some inquiries." Jordan looked very relaxed. "Don't worry, Alan, that hasn't anything to do with my coming to see you."

"So why have you?"

"Because I want you to come to my party."

"To keep an eye on the spoons?"

Jordan laughed. "If it was that I'd have hired you, not sent you an invitation."

"Invitations come cheaper. I may have been a bit wet behind the ears when I was at school—"

"Weren't we all?"

"You weren't. I've learnt a lot since then— and I've heard a lot of dodgy stories. It's something to do with that cutting, isn't it?"

"I wondered when we'd get round to that," Jordan remarked evenly. "You've read it?"

"Yes."

"I thought you might be interested."

He's setting me up, Craig told himself. I don't know why or what it's all about, but he's planning something and he means me to be a part of it. The thought made him vaguely uneasy.

"Why did you send it?" he demanded.

"I told you, I thought you'd be interested." Jordan seemed to dismiss the cutting. "You'll come to my party, won't you? I'd very much like you to be there."

Craig saw that now, at least, he was sincere. For some reason Micky badly wanted him to say he'd come.

"Why?" he asked again. "Why me?"

Jordan smiled. "Because you're you."

"I'm not going to be anybody's monkey, mate."

"My dear chap, I wouldn't ask you for that. You can take it as a compliment I want you to come. Sincerely."

Hooey, Craig thought. "Who else will be there?" he asked.

"Only a few friends. Don't worry, they're all quite normal—and except for Simon Fenn, who's a writer, none of them is in television."

"All right, I'll come," Craig told him. He sounded as if he had just come to a decision but he knew he had made up his mind some time ago. "I don't know why, and I'm probably a fool, but I will."

"Thanks, Alan." Something surprisingly like relief showed in Jordan's tone. Then he asked easily, "How's the business going? Are you getting much work?"

"Not much," Craig admitted.

"I might be able to help there." Jordan glanced at his watch and stood up. "I must go. They've given me a new producer for the next series and there are a lot of angles to sort out. He must be the chairman's nephew or something. God knows how he got the job otherwise, he's a complete moron. See you about six on the Friday."

"Okay," Craig said.

"'Bye, Alan. It really has been great to see you again." Jordan held out his hand.

"And you," Craig agreed, shaking it. He couldn't have cared less, he thought.

When he had seen Jordan out he closed the door and sat down at his desk. What was Micky up to? He had been too keen for him to go to his party and too relieved when he said he would. It must be something to do with that old murder case, the casual way he had dismissed the cutting when Craig mentioned it wouldn't have deceived a child, but what was it?

Picking up his phone, Craig dialled the number of a journalist he knew. Experience had taught him that doing your homework properly could save a lot of grief later, and he had a feeling that that included learning all he could about Jordan.

2

LOWER MARKING had changed very little in the last fifty years. True, many of the old cottages had been modernised and were now occupied by professional people who commuted to the towns to work rather than by the old village families, but most of the post-war building, a small council estate and an even smaller private development, was on the outskirts of the village or tucked away down a turning off the High Street from which the neo-Georgian houses were hardly visible. The street itself was brighter and looked more cared for, otherwise it was almost exactly as it must have been in 1939.

When Craig drove along it a bus had just pulled up outside the village hall and people were alighting from it. Apart from them the short street was deserted. He saw an Early English church with a squat tower, thirty or forty cottages interspersed with a handful of larger houses, and three or four shops. Then, round a shady corner he came to a traffic derestriction sign and Lower Marking was behind him.

The White House was half a mile beyond the village. Built by a local banker in the early 19th century, it was not large but it was well proportioned, with white walls under a slate roof and a verandah, roofed and embellished with graceful iron pillars, running the whole width of the front.

You approached the house, which was almost hidden from the road, from the south-east. On the west it was shaded by a magnificent cedar of Lebanon and to the south the ground sloped gently away to a valley. Driving up that slope between massed rhododendrons, Craig wondered how long Jordan had lived here. It was hard to imagine any of his other school-mates in these surroundings but, looking back now, there had always been something about Micky which suggested he would succeed.

The temperature had been in the low eighties since this morning and, although it was a little cooler now, the house still seemed to be basking in a shimmering haze. As he stopped his elderly Triumph Dolomite Sprint Craig experienced again the vague uneasiness he had felt before. He didn't know what Micky planned, nor why he had wanted him to come so badly, but he couldn't rid himself of the suspicion that if he had known he wouldn't have liked it.

He rang the old fashioned bell and after a brief pause it was answered by a pleasant looking middle-aged woman in a grey dress.

"I'm Alan Craig," he told her.

"Yes, of course, Mr. Craig. I'm Mrs. Davies, Mr. Jordan's housekeeper." She stood aside for him to step into the hall.

Craig's case hadn't been a good one when it was new, now it was shabby to the point of being disreputable. He put it down and looked round. The hall was long and rather narrow in proportion to its length, the walls Adam green and the woodwork white. There were three modern landscapes on the walls and a bowl of crimson roses on a Sheraton sofa table under one of them. It was a cool, elegant hall. He had been in others very like it, but never as a guest.

Mrs. Davies stooped to pick up his case, but Craig beat her to it. Smiling, she led the way up a wide, gracefully curving staircase.

"Mr. Jordan's very sorry," she said, "but he's been delayed in London. He'll be here in time for dinner."

Craig's room was at the end of the landing

24

on the right. It was large and airy, and when the housekeeper had gone he walked over to the window and looked out. Beyond the spreading branches of the great cedar he could see a swimming pool, deserted now, and, farther to the left, the neat rectangle of a tennis court, its asphalt surface patterned with white lines. He knew without being told that beyond the court, past the lawns and the flowerbeds, the ground sloped away towards a wood with a stream flowing past its other side.

Suddenly his uneasiness became more pronounced, and he was conscious of a sense of foreboding.

As he turned away from the window he heard another car drive up and stop in front of the house. Doors slammed metallically, not quite in unison, and footsteps crunched on the gravel. Wondering who the new arrivals might be, Craig started taking off his jacket.

When he had washed and changed he eyed his reflection in the mirror. Was his lightweight grey-brown suit all right? Neither too formal nor too informal? Whatever they said, people like Micky Jordan judged you by your appearance as much as any old Blimp of a colonel, and they were the first to curl the old lip if you didn't conform to their standards. Well, if his gear was all wrong, that was too bad, he was the one who was doing a favour by coming here, and they could take him as he was or do the other thing, he didn't care.

But Craig wasn't deceiving himself, he knew he was afraid he would be out of place here. He had never been at his ease with people who let him see they considered themselves his superiors.

The others probably knew each other already, Micky had said they were friends, and he would be the odd one out. They would talk about television and the theatre and subjects he didn't understand and which didn't interest him. He had been a fool to allow himself to be talked into coming simply on the strength of having been at school with Micky twenty years ago. It wasn't as if they had been particular friends even then. He must want his head examining.

No, he told himself, be fair. He had come because he was curious, just as Georgie had predicted he would. He might have felt better if Georgie were here now. The thought of her in these surroundings made him grin.

He stepped out on to the landing. It was very quiet. Craig wasn't used to such quiet in a house, his own home over the shop in Streatham had been cramped and never quite silent, even at night, while his present flat was above another shared by three noisy girl students. The quiet here was restful, yet at the same time slightly disconcerting.

He started towards the stairs, wondering if the other guests had arrived by now and were beyond the closed doors he passed. As he reached the top of the stairs he heard a woman in a room on his right say, "If I'd known I would never have come. I wouldn't." Her voice was pitched high with distress—or fear.

Another woman asked in an American accent, "Why not, honey? You surely don't believe in ghosts, do you? It was all so long ago, there's nothing for you to worry about."

Craig went on down the stairs. The hall was deserted but he could hear voices through the open door of a room on his left and he walked across to it.

There were six people in the room. They didn't notice him immediately and he stood just inside the door watching them. Jordan was in the centre of the group with a slim girl in her early twenties wearing a white dress on his right. She had a rather rectangular face with a square jaw and naturally blonde hair hanging to her bare shoulders, but the feature Craig noticed first was her eyes. Their calm, thoughtful expression and a hint of sadness in them lent her something very like beauty, although she was by no means conventionally pretty.

The others were a tall, thin elderly man, slightly stooped and with a fringe of grey hair; a gaunt woman of about the same age with handsome, rather autocratic features; a weedy, dark man a good deal younger, and an over-ripe Mediterranean beauty with a sulky mouth and a bored look.

Then Jordan saw Craig and came to meet him, pulling the girl with him. Surely she couldn't be his wife? Craig thought. According to Dooley, the source of most of his information about Jordan, Sandra Jordan had been a nurse before she married him five years ago. This girl looked too young.

"Alan!" Jordan exclaimed. "Come in and meet everybody. This is Gail Lakeland. Darling, meet Alan Craig, a very old friend of mine."

The girl said "Hallo" and gave Craig a rather reserved smile.

"Elizabeth and Charles Laxton. Simon and Gabriella Fenn."

Craig realised why the tall man's face had seemed vaguely familiar, he had seen photographs of Laxton in the papers and watched him on television. He had little sympathy for the MP's views, but he knew Laxton was the sort of politician of whom many of his former colleagues approved, he talked a good deal about law and order and protecting the public, as if they were benefits you could turn on like a tap. His wife had a long, thin nose and lips to match. Her eyes were cold and she generated an air of well bred fastidiousness.

Seen at close quarters the Fenns were very different. He was intense and looked as if he lived at the edge of his nerves, Gabriella looked sulky and was almost certainly interested only in herself. Craig was more interested in their name.

"I'm sorry I wasn't here when you all arrived," Jordan was saying. "I couldn't get away from a God-awful meeting about the new series. You've no idea how appalling these people can be. What'll you have to drink, Alan?"

Craig was tempted to ask for a pint of beer,

partly because he was thirsty, but also as the gesture he felt he owed it to himself to make, but he suspected that if he did the other guests would regard him with even more contempt than they did already, so he said, "A gin and tonic, please."

"Where have you come from, Craig?" Laxton asked him.

Craig understood it was a not very subtle attempt to discover where he lived and, by implication, his background.

"London," he answered. Make something of that, he thought.

Jordan handed him his drink and he sipped it, savouring the tingle of the tonic on his tongue and the chill of the ice. The conversation was desultory, as if the others had only just met and were still groping for topics of mutual interest.

Craig had a sudden strange feeling that they were all waiting for something to happen. Perhaps they didn't know why they had been invited any more than he did. Or perhaps it was only for the arrival of the last guests, for there was no noticeable tension in the room. Only Laxton kept frowning, as if something were puzzling him.

Gabriella Fenn had succeeded in detaching her host from Gail Lakeland and was clearly intent on monopolising his attention while her husband watched balefully.

"I've been here before, you know, Jordan," Laxton remarked, stimulated perhaps by his second or third large gin. "I knew it as soon as I saw the house."

"Oh?" Jordan's tone was politely interested.

"Must be over twenty years ago. It wasn't called The White House then, it was some man's name. Damned if I can remember it now."

"Bensons." It was a woman's voice, husky and with an American accent, just behind Craig. The voice he had heard on the landing.

They all turned. Two women were standing in the doorway. They were both middle-aged and both expensively dressed, but there any likeness ended. The taller had fair, untidy hair and a rather vacant face with small, deep set eyes. She was stout and looked uncomfortable in her dress, which was too young for her. Or perhaps her unease was caused by something else, Craig thought, remembering the snatch of conversation he had heard upstairs.

Her companion was a golden blonde, elegant

and immaculately groomed with everything calculated to enhance her beauty. For she was still undeniably beautiful and, although her figure was no longer quite as slim as it had been ten years ago, she carried herself so well and moved so gracefully that a casual observer hardly noticed the change. She was wearing a good deal of make-up and diamonds sparkled at her throat and ears and on her long, scarlet-tipped fingers. But it was not only her appearance you noticed, she possessed a vitality, a radiance, even, that was evident even when she was still. Beside her the other woman looked faded and insignificant.

Lorraine Maxwell, the film star, Craig told himself, staring at her and hardly believing it. After beginning to make a name for herself, first on the stage, then in two or three indifferent British films in the Fifties, she had gone to Hollywood, and within a few years her name was a household word. Her three marriages—and three subsequent divorces—had made headlines over half the world, yet she seemed to be immune to the scandal other stars attracted. In an age when the words themselves were passé she was still a film star. Craig remembered what Georgie had said about not knowing who might be here. She hadn't known the half of it.

"My God!" Laxton breathed. "Lorraine!"

"Hallo, Charles darling." The actress smiled warmly at him. "You remember Caroline, don't you?"

Laxton gazed at the fair woman as if she were a ghost. "You too!" he exclaimed.

Lorraine laughed quietly. "I must say, that's not very gallant of you, Charles."

Whether she had intended it or not, her advance into the room was undeniably an "entrance". Putting her hands on Jordan's shoulders, she kissed him affectionately. "Miles darling."

"Hallo, Lorraine. It's lovely of you to come. And you, Caroline. I was just saying how sorry I was I couldn't be here when you all arrived. I got held up at the studios."

Jordan introduced the two women to the other people in the room while they stood, a trifle awkwardly, waiting until he had seen the newcomers were supplied with drinks.

Then Lorraine Maxwell asked, "Did you know this house used to be called Bensons, Miles?"

"No," he said. "Really? It was The White

House when I bought it. Have you been here before as well?"

"Oh yes. Caroline and Charles and I, we've all been here before."

"They probably changed the name after what happened," Laxton remarked.

"What did happen?" Gabriella asked. Perhaps she realised she could no longer monopolise her host's attention and was determined not to be overlooked.

"A woman shot her husband at a party here," the MP told her. "A woman named Susan Randall. It was their place. She was a bit . . ." He stopped.

"A bit what?" Jordan enquired casually.

The others were listening intently and Craig sensed that some of them were on edge. He wondered why. Was it only that unpleasant memories were being revived or was there more to it?

"There were other men," Laxton answered. "And he had other women. It was a sordid business altogether."

Craig was watching Jordan and he was almost certain he saw him tense. His conviction that Micky had arranged this party for some reason that had nothing to do with the company of friends or normal hospitality returned and he had a sudden bizarre notion that perhaps there were microphones and television cameras hidden outside the room, recording everything that was said and done here. But surely even Jordan wouldn't try to get away with that?

So what was he up to?

Beside Craig Gail Lakeland had suppressed a gasp. She didn't relish the idea of a murder having been committed here, he thought.

"Where did it happen?" she asked.

"In the summerhouse by the river," Laxton told her. "Is it still there, Jordan?"

"Yes."

Craig noticed that Lorraine Maxwell was watching her host with an oddly calculating expression. She, too, was wondering what he had planned, he thought.

"What happened to her?" Gail asked in a breathless voice.

"She was reprieved," Laxton said curtly. It was clear that, having raised the subject, he now wanted to drop it as quickly as possible.

"You don't approve, Charles?" Jordan asked him lightly. "Of her being reprieved, I mean. But you wouldn't, would you? You're a great believer in the gallows."

"I'm in favour of the return of capital punishment for certain categories of murder, if that's what you mean," the MP acknowledged stiffly. "It's necessary to protect the public."

"And what about crucifying the poor bastard's family for what he did?" Jordan asked, his tone no longer bantering. "Always assuming you've got the right man in the first place—and God knows how you can be sure of that. You think that's all right? Because that's what you'd do, Charles. Who do you think you'd be punishing the most, the murderer or his family? They would be condemned to wait, with everybody watching them, for the day when the law took him out, trussed like a dummy, and hanged him by the neck, and they knew they couldn't even hope any more. They would have to live with his being in the condemned cell, imagining what he was going through. After a few weeks it would all be over for him, but they would have to go on living with it. Remembering. What right have you to make innocent people suffer like that? And what if he wasn't guilty after all? You couldn't bring him back and say you were sorry, you'd made a mistake. The trouble with people like you isn't that you're deliberately cruel, it's that you lack the slightest trace of imagination."

"That point of view's sentimental. Emotional," Laxton said angrily. A touch of colour stained his pale cheeks.

"No, Charles, it's your argument that's based on emotion; you believe in revenge, an eye for an eye and a tooth for a tooth."

Jordan's manner had become accusing, and when he finished there was an embarrassed silence. Laxton had flushed darker, and although his wife said nothing, she was clearly furious. Lorraine Maxwell was eyeing Jordan as if what he had said disturbed her, and Fenn was staring at him in a startled way. Gail Lakeland looked uncomfortable. Only Gabriella appeared unaffected.

Jordan broke the silence himself. "I apologise, Charles," he said. "That was an unforgivable way to behave to a guest. I'm afraid you got me on one of my hobby-horses."

"Do we have to talk about it?" Caroline demanded petulantly. She had gone very pale and her make-up stood out in unlovely blotches. She looked, Craig thought, as if she was about to faint. "I'm sure nobody is interested in what happened all those years ago."

"I'm sorry, I am," Jordan told her. He might have been craving her indulgence for some rather attractive foible. "After all, this is my home now. But I promise I won't worry you with it this evening."

The woman looked slightly mollified, but Craig, who was beginning to suspect that Jordan did and said nothing without a reason, wondered if there was any significance in his saying "this evening" rather than "this week-end."

"It was all a long time ago," Lorraine said. "I guess Charles only mentioned it because, the three of us meeting again like this, he couldn't help remembering. It's so long since we saw each other."

"Not since the trial," Laxton agreed, then looked as if he wished he hadn't spoken.

"Sure. And Miles didn't even know we knew each other, did you, darling?"

"How could I?" Jordan smiled disarmingly.

You're lying, Craig thought.

Another awkward silence was averted by the housekeeper's coming in and informing Jordan that dinner was ready.

He looked round at them. "Shall we go in?" he asked.

Craig found himself sitting on Gail Lakeland's right. She was at one end of the oval table, facing Jordan, and Craig wondered if Sandra was merely away or if she and Micky had separated. He and Gail seemed to be more than friends, but Craig knew that in his business displays of affection often meant very little. On his right was Caroline Rogers who, he was satisfied, had been Caroline Bateman when she gave evidence at Susan Randall's trial. She virtually ignored him, and as Gail's other neighbour, Simon Fenn, was giving all his attention to Lorraine Maxwell, they talked to each other a good deal of the time.

She told him little about herself except that she was a publisher's publicity manager, from which he supposed she was older than he had thought. Once, when they were discussing holidays, he mentioned that he had toured in Spain the previous year and asked her if she knew the country. She answered rather brusquely that she didn't and that Spain had never appealed to her. The abruptness of her answer to a perfectly normal question surprised Craig and he wondered if Spain had unpleasant associations for her. Perhaps she realised she had spoken curtly, for afterwards her manner became as friendly as it had been before.

Apparently the general uneasiness before dinner had been forgotten, the atmosphere round the table was relaxed and the hum of conversation almost unbroken. Not quite, however, and there was a sudden silence just as Gail asked Craig, "Why do you call Miles 'Micky'?"

Craig knew that everybody was looking at him and he hesitated before he answered, wondering whether in telling them he would in a small way be betraying Jordan. Maybe Micky didn't want people to know that he had been at a comprehensive school and that his name wasn't really Miles.

"I've wondered that too," Gabriella chimed in, succeeding in endowing the words with a proprietorial tone which deceived nobody.

Craig saw a slight smile twitching the corners of Jordan's mouth. "I've known him a long time," he said. "Since we were kids."

"We were at school together," Jordan explained. "My real name's Michael, but when I started in television I changed it. There were so many Michaels already. And I could imagine the snide remarks about St. Michael and the Jordan."

"Weren't you presuming rather a lot?" Fenn suggested. "*Saint* Michael?" There was sufficient malice in his tone to slightly embarrass the other people round the table.

"You think so?" Jordan spoke good humouredly. "Perhaps you're right."

"Who was St. Michael?" Gail asked. "Apart from being a label, I mean."

"The guardian angel of the Jews," Fenn told her.

"Don't forget he led the angels against Satan too, Simon," Jordan said drily.

Fenn eyed him strangely. "I'll watch out," he promised.

Everybody else was eyeing them uncomfortably.

"When I was in *Snakes in Heaven* with Spencer Tracy," Lorraine said as if she had been in the middle of a story when she was interrupted and speaking rather loudly. "Tracy was a lovely man and a wonderful actor, but that day . . ."

It was a long story and extremely funny and she told it well, holding their attention by the strength of her personality, sparkling like the

41

diamonds she was wearing and using her lovely voice to the best effect as she mimicked actors and directors. By the time she finished the whole party was laughing and the moment's uneasiness had passed.

"Who is Fenn?" Craig asked Gail when the other man's attention was again concentrated on Lorraine.

"He's an author."

"I know; Micky said something."

"He wrote two or three quite good novels and one or two things for radio and Miles asked him to work on a couple of his programmes." Gail hesitated. "I never knew quite why, his stuff wasn't in Miles' line at all."

Craig thought that the reason was obvious, but that it would be tactless to suggest it. Anyway, he was more interested in Jordan's motive for inviting Fenn here this weekend, and the writer's for accepting when he made no secret of his feelings for his host. Or were Fenn's barbed remarks less malicious than they sounded? The spontaneous shots of a man who felt impelled to be clever at all costs. There were plenty of men like that, but Craig doubted if Fenn were one of them. Moreover one reason for his dislike was only too apparent. Craig looked along the table to where Gabriella was doing her best to keep Jordan's attention firmly fixed on her.

He realised Gail was asking him a question. "Sorry?" he said.

"I asked what you did."

Craig hesitated. "Until a few weeks ago I was in the police," he replied.

"You aren't now?"

"No."

Jordan had heard them. "Alan's a detective," he said.

Craig wondered why they all with the exception of Lorraine Maxwell and Gail seemed startled. Lorraine was regarding him with the same calculating expression he had observed before dinner when she was looking at Jordan.

"I'm not here professionally," he said lightly.

"No, of course not." Jordan's tone made the confirmation sound more like a contradiction.

"That's what you say," Caroline Rogers said, her rather penetrating voice pitched higher than usual. "How do we know it's true?"

"You don't," Jordan told her. "But would it worry you if it weren't?"

Caroline looked flustered. "No. No, of course not," she said. "Why should it?"

"I've no idea." Jordan smiled.

All the same, Craig told himself, for some reason the possibility had alarmed Caroline. For a few seconds she had looked almost frightened. There were too many under-currents here, too much tension just below the surface. What game was Micky playing?

The uneasiness didn't last long. Lorraine Maxwell, apparently unwilling to have their attention leave her for long, started telling another outrageous story, talking a little too loudly and her American accent more marked. Craig eyed her curiously.

The rest of the evening passed without incident. Jordan rather monopolised Gail and Craig felt himself isolated. He told himself it was only what he had expected: why the hell had Micky wanted him to come?

3

THE next morning dawned fine and warm with a light haze. Craig was the first of the guests down. During his time in the CID he had had to school himself to snatch sleep as and when he could and now, when there was no need for him to be about for at least another hour, he woke before seven and found it impossible to sleep any more.

Washed and dressed and taking care to disturb no one, he went downstairs. From the back of the house came the sounds of somebody moving about, but he saw no one as he let himself out and turned left along the verandah. Beyond the house was a large gravelled rectangle enclosed on three sides by outbuildings, the largest of which, a mellow red brick building with white painted window frames and a tiled roof darkened by patches of moss, must once have been the stable block. The stables themselves had been converted into a large garage and, or so Craig assumed from the curtains at the windows, the coachman's

45

quarters over them into a flat, now, presumably, occupied by Mrs. Davies—and her husband if she had one.

Behind the house there was an extensive kitchen garden with meticulously weeded rows of plants and two large greenhouses. Wondering if Micky grew grapes and produced his own wine, Craig walked on to the far end of the house, rounded it, and came to the swimming pool. It was large enough to have satisfied the most exhibitionist Hollywood star, surrounded by a wide tiled area and overlooked by a row of three French windows. On its other side there was a small copse with a wall beyond it.

Craig turned and walked back the way he had come. From the garage a path led round the side of the lawn to the eastern end of the wood, but he ignored it and walked across the close cropped turf to a pergola, almost bowed under the weight of pink climbing roses, midway along the other side of the lawn. It was short, little more than a rustic arch, and beyond it and a narrow strip of orchard he came to the wood.

So early in the morning the sun wasn't strong enough to penetrate the dense foliage and it was half dark under the trees, while the air was cool and had a pleasant musty odour. Craig was on a path of trodden earth and leaf mould. It must have been somewhere here, he told himself, that Caroline and Rupert Bateman had met Susan Randall looking for her husband that fateful July afternoon exactly thirty years ago. Now there was no sign of anyone.

The silence made the crack of the shot sound louder than it was. At the same moment something slammed into a tree a few feet from where Craig was standing. He turned, startled.

"What the . . . ?" he ejaculated.

What crazy fool was letting off a gun without making sure there was nobody in range? The report hadn't sounded like that of a shot-gun, he thought. More like a ·22 rifle.

Craig didn't know much about poachers, they rarely came within the orbit of a detective sergeant in the inner divisions of the Met, but he doubted whether they made a habit of wandering about in woods at eight o'clock in the morning firing indiscriminately.

While he was still debating whether to challenge the marksman or to dive to the ground in case he fired again, there was a rustle of undergrowth and a remarkable figure appeared on the path twenty yards ahead of him. The newcomer was a small, wiry man of about forty-five with black hair and a puckish face. He was wearing denim shorts, wellingtons and, despite the warmth of the morning, a grubby old raincoat which, hanging open, revealed a gaily checked sports shirt. Over his left shoulder he was carrying a light-weight rifle.

"Who are you?" Craig demanded.

The man regarded him with cheery self-assurance. "I might ask you the same, boyo," he retorted in a broad Welsh accent.

"I'm staying here."

"So you say. You look more like a copper to me."

Craig was beginning to be annoyed. "Would it worry you if I was."

"Worry me? No, boyo. Why should it? I just don't like coppers, that's all."

"Well, I'm not a copper. Who are you?"

"My name's Willy Davies. I'm the gardener here."

"What were you shooting at?"

"Pigeons. They eat my vegetables, see."

"Why don't you use a shot-gun?"

"Not me." The little Welshman looked disgusted. "Nasty noisy things they are. I don't like them. A two-two's a proper gun."

Craig remembered that a bullet hadn't missed

him by very much. "You're not much of a shot," he remarked with feeling, although his anger was fading fast. "You nearly hit me."

"You? It was miles from you." Davies grinned. "But I will say I didn't expect to find one of his nibs' guests about at this time of the morning. Mostly they aren't up before nine. Oh well, I'll be off to my breakfast, boyo."

Nodding cheerfully, the gardener dived into the trees on the other side of the path. Craig could hear the trampling of leaves and the occasional snap of a twig that marked his progress and in spite of his indignation he grinned. He was quite sure Davies had been taking the mickey out of him, but there was something about the perky little Welshman that defied him to be angry.

The wood extended for another eighty yards or so. In some places the undergrowth was quite dense, in others there was none and Craig could see some distance between the trees. Then, quite suddenly, the trees ended and he emerged on to a grassy terrace overlooking the river which here was some twenty yards wide. Though it flowed slowly, there was very little weed. In the distance Craig could see the bridge which carried the road from the village over it, while nearer at hand a family of ducks was paddling busily upstream.

A little way to his right was a summerhouse, a solid octagonal structure of rough logs with a pointed roof facing the river. He walked over to it. The only window was on the other side and there was no door, only a small open area with an opening leading to the single room. It faced south-west and at this time of the morning little light reached the interior. Apart from a small, battered table and an upright chair, it was empty, but it looked as if it had been cleaned and swept recently and Craig wondered if Jordan sometimes worked here.

Perhaps it was the semi-darkness. Or the slight chill. It seemed to Craig that the summer-house possessed an atmosphere which was not so much sinister as vaguely depressing. It wasn't difficult to remember that a man had been murdered here, shot down in cold blood by his wife.

Craig turned and walked back to the house.

With the exception of Gabriella Fenn, who was having something taken up to her in bed, the guests were gathered in the breakfast-room. When Craig walked in Caroline Rogers was asking Jordan in a querulous voice, "What is all this about, Miles? Why have you asked us all here?"

Jordan smiled easily. "You're all my friends, dear."

"You're up to something."

"Up to something?"

"It was this weekend Susan shot Nigel, the 17th July, and three of us were here then. You can't tell me that's just coincidence."

"What do you mean?" Fenn demanded. He sounded more on edge than he had done last night and Craig wondered if he and Gabriella had quarrelled and if that was the reason for her non-appearance this morning.

"Nothing, Simon," Lorraine Maxwell told him. "Miles isn't up to anything."

Jordan regarded her quizzically. "Oh, but I am," he said.

"You see?" Fenn demanded.

Jordan smiled.

"Look here," Charles Laxton began. "You invited us here and—" His wife nudged him and he stopped.

"You think I'm abusing a host's privilege?" Jordan asked. "I assure you, Charles, I'm not. Not yet, at least."

"Then what is it all about?" Fenn insisted.

"You'll see in good time, Simon. But do believe me, you have nothing to worry about."

Later Craig was to wonder if he had imagined a slight emphasis on that "you".

"When?" Laxton wanted to know.

"Tomorrow. I don't know why you all look so concerned, it's only a sort of game." He paused and looked round at them. "Does anybody feel like tennis this morning?"

Nobody displayed much enthusiasm, but after breakfast a four was arranged and they went to change.

Craig played with Fenn against Jordan and Gail. He and Jordan were reasonable club players and Gail could have held her own against either of them; Fenn had consented to play reluctantly to make up the four and he was little better than a passenger. From the start it was obvious that his mind wasn't on the game and he soon became petulant, arguing over line calls, then lapsing into moody silences. Craig found it hard to contain his irritation, he didn't mind playing with somebody who wasn't much good, but he resented a partner whose every move proclaimed that he had no intention of trying.

Fenn's resentment seemed to be directed at

his host but Jordan was at his friendliest and refused to let it ruffle him.

"For God's sake!" Gail exclaimed angrily at one point. And when at the end of the second set Craig asked if the others wanted to play a third, she replied bitterly, "No, thank you," and walked off.

Jordan watched her go, muttered something Craig didn't catch, and went after her. But he made no attempt to catch her up and when she reached the house he was still some way behind her. Craig strolled towards the other members of the party who were sitting in deck-chairs on the lawn and sat down in an empty chair beside Elizabeth Laxton.

"If one agrees to play, one should try," she remarked.

"I'm sorry?" Craig said. "You mean me?"

"No, of course not. Simon Fenn."

"He had his mind on something else."

"That was obvious."

Craig let it pass, Fenn's preoccupations were no concern of his.

"How long has Miles had this house?" Lorraine enquired casually.

"I don't know," Caroline Rogers answered.

She looked worried this morning, Craig thought.

"Not long, I gather," Laxton said. "Where did you meet him, Lorrie?"

"In New York. I was doing a play on Broadway and he was at a party somebody gave. When he knew I planned to come over to England soon he said he hoped we'd meet again like anyone does, you know? Then when I got here, he sent me an invitation for this weekend. It was kind of sweet of him; I'd lost touch with everybody I used to know over here. It's seven years since I came to England the last time and then it was only for a few days."

"Why did you stay away so long?" Elizabeth asked.

"I don't know. I was busy and I just never got around to doing anything about it, I guess. Do you watch his show on television?"

"Occasionally." Elizabeth's tone was non-committal.

"What's it like?"

"He's clever." Laxton sounded judicial, almost grudging. "You can't argue about that. I can't say I like his style though, all this fashionable sniping at things just because they're old. He's Left wing, of course. All these fellows are."

"He's dangerous," Elizabeth said, her mouth clamping tight.

"He takes pleasure in destroying things," Fenn, who had joined them, said surprisingly.

"Like hypocrisy and conceit?" Lorraine suggested.

Fenn laughed harshly. "If you believe that, you don't know him. He's not fit to mix with normal people."

There was something rather shocking about the raw bitterness in the author's voice, and for a few seconds nobody spoke. Then Elizabeth observed coldly, "I'm surprised you came."

"Don't think I wanted to," Fenn told her. He stood up abruptly and walked off towards the house.

"What's up with him?" Laxton asked.

"Gabriella?" Caroline murmured. "She doesn't exactly hide it, does she?" She picked up a magazine from the grass beside her chair and began glancing idly at the pages.

"No," Elizabeth agreed. "Can she really be as stupid as that?"

It was a question no one attempted to answer.

After a few minutes Lorraine announced that she was chilly and was going to fetch a jacket.

"Chilly?" Laxton stared at her. "It's over eighty, you can't be chilly."

"I guess I've lived in California too long, Charles," Lorraine said.

Craig watched her stroll away and cross the verandah. It was impossible to guess what she was thinking behind those beautifully enamelled features, he thought. At dinner last night she had played the film star role hard when things looked like becoming awkward, today she was much quieter and her manner more restrained. He suspected that she was not only a beautiful woman and a fine actress, but intelligent and perceptive too. Whatever her real reason for leaving them now, he was sure she would be wearing a jacket when she returned.

He waited a minute or so, then muttered an excuse and followed her. As he passed the open window of the morning room which overlooked the verandah he saw her in the room and heard her say, "Okay, if that's how it is."

"That's how it is," Jordan's voice agreed.

"You're a fool, Miles. You know that?"

"You're free to think so."

Craig walked on into the house. As he crossed

the hall, making for the stairs, a door on the right opened and Lorraine came out. For a second or two her guard was down and he saw concern—perhaps even fear—on her face. Then she noticed him, forced a smile, and went quickly up the stairs.

Craig hesitated for a moment, then entered the room she had just left. Jordan was looking out of the window, but when he heard the door close he turned.

"Oh, it's you," he said. His tone seemed to imply that he had been expecting somebody else.

"I want to know what's going on, Micky," Craig told him.

"You too?" Jordan smiled. "Why does everybody think there's something going on?"

"You know why: you mean them to. You said yourself you're up to something."

"I'm beginning to think that was a mistake. I just couldn't resist it when Simon started getting neurotic and Lorraine tried to soothe him down."

Craig reflected that Micky had been the same at school, given to acting on sudden mischievous impulses. But he wasn't going to be deflected from his purpose now.

"What is it?" he demanded.

"I told you," Jordan said. "A sort of game."

"Like murder?" Craig suggested.

There was a second's pause before Jordan said lightly, "What on earth makes you say that? Of course not."

"Stop it, Micky."

"Considering you don't know what it is you think I'm planning, how can you tell me to stop it?" Jordan's tone had changed, the bantering note had gone.

"Because I'm pretty sure it's dangerous. And it's not your field."

"You're coming over all dramatic like the others. There's nothing dangerous. And it is my field, as you call it. I'm a journalist. Remember?"

"Then you ought to be able to sense the atmosphere," Craig told him.

"The trouble with policemen—and ex-policemen apparently," Jordan remarked with an edge to his voice, "is that they see crime everywhere. They're so tiresomely suspicious."

"So why did you invite me?" Craig demanded.

"If I said for old times' sake, you wouldn't believe me."

58

"Too right I wouldn't."

"Let's leave it then."

Craig saw that he was going to get no more out of his host and he turned towards the door. He was halfway to it when Jordan said, "Don't worry, I meant it when I said there was nothing for you to be concerned about. How could there be?"

Craig didn't know, but a sudden thought occurred to him. "Is Davies part of it?" he asked.

"Davies? Willy Davies, you mean?" Jordan looked genuinely puzzled.

"Yes. He was in the wood with a two-two this morning. He nearly shot me."

"You can be sure he didn't mean to hit you then; Willy's a first class shot."

"Thanks very much."

"Did you speak to him?"

"What do you think?"

"What did he say?"

"That he was after pigeons."

Jordan laughed. "He's always on about them. Willy's a fanatic about the gardens and he says they eat things."

"He's a fanatic all right—if by that you mean

he's round the twist," Craig said warmly. "Next time he might be lucky and hit somebody."

"I expect he'll be more careful in future. He's not used to people staying here being about so early. Poor Willy, he's had a hard time."

"It'll be harder if he's not careful, he'll end up in gaol."

"He used to work at the studios. There was an accident, some heavy scenery fell on one of the other men and he was nearly killed. The trouble was, the chap had been messing about with Willy's wife—his first wife, not Joan. Willy didn't have anything to do with the accident, but there was a lot of talk and your old mates gave him a rough time." Jordan paused. "You can take my word for it, Alan, Willy hasn't anything to do with my game."

The telephone rang and he picked it up. Craig started towards the door. As he reached it he heard Jordan say, "Oh, it's you. Hallo . . . Must we? . . . Very well then . . ."

He went out, closing the door behind him.

4

DURING lunch Jordan said, "I'm afraid there's some work I must do this afternoon. I'm sorry, it's hardly being the perfect host, but Gail will look after you as well as I could."

The blonde girl was watching him with a puzzled little frown.

"It's this new series," Jordan explained to the Laxtons. "It's going to be different from the others—more investigative—and there's an awful lot of work to do. We're behind schedule and the gods are making disapproving noises."

"What will you be investigating?" Elizabeth asked. The question sounded innocent enough, but Craig didn't miss the hard undertone.

"Political scandals, miscarriages of justice, all sorts of things," Jordan replied, smiling. "I hope you'll tell me if you know of anything that might make a good programme."

Nobody said anything.

After lunch the sky was still a cloudless blue. Lying on a sun lounger beside the pool Craig felt the heat scorching his skin. A bee hummed past, and from somewhere behind the wall bordering the little copse came the purr of a lawnmower. Warm, relaxing sounds, he thought. Could a sound be warm? A cabbage white butterfly fluttered near, and it occurred to him that he wouldn't give much for its chances if Willy Davies saw it.

Had Micky been wholly frank about Davies? Craig suspected that there had been more to the accident at the studios than he had told him.

He was aware of an uneasy restlessness. It was like the feeling he had had before dinner last night, that all of them were waiting for something to happen. Was that why Jordan had asked him here?

Beside him Gail stirred and turned over.

"Have you known Micky long?" Craig asked her.

"About three months. He wanted one of our authors to appear on his programme and I tried to set it up. In the end nothing came of it." Gail raised her head a couple of inches to look at Craig. "In case you're wondering, his marriage was breaking up before I met him."

"I wasn't."

"Oh. You're not married?"

"No. I was once."

"You're divorced?"

"No." Why did he still find it hard to talk about Jean? Craig wondered. To say she was dead? Was it because putting it into words made her death more real, more final? A youth in a car, showing off to his girl, taking one risk too many, and in seconds two lives were shattered. The boy had escaped with minor cuts and bruises.

That had been five months ago and the wounds were still raw.

Twenty yards away the Fenns looked as if they were asleep.

"My wife's dead," Craig said quietly.

"Oh, I'm sorry." They were conventional words and they might have been empty, but Gail sounded as if she meant them. With a single graceful movement she sat up. "Let's play tennis," she said.

"It's too hot," Craig protested.

"I'll go mad if I just lie here not knowing . . ."

"Not knowing what?"

"Nothing. Come on." Gail picked up her racquet and the bag of balls and set off towards the court.

Not too reluctantly Craig followed her.

He won the first set 6–4, and as they changed ends for the second he glanced across at the lawn. There was no sign of Caroline but Lorraine and the Laxtons were still reclining in their deck chairs. He looked farther round to his left. Gabriella was sitting on the edge of the pool, dangling her feet in the water, but Fenn was no longer with her. Then Craig saw him on the verandah, walking in the direction of the old stables.

"Why did you leave the police?" Gail enquired when they met at the net. "Or is that a rude question?"

"No. My dad had a newsagent's and tobacconist's. He died six months ago and left it to me. I'd already decided it was time I left the Force, but I couldn't face spending the rest of my life serving behind a counter. The only job I knew anything about was police work. I reckoned there must be an opening for somebody who was prepared to work hard and give people a good service, so I sold the shop and used the money to set up an agency: Alan Craig Associates."

"How long had you been in the police?"

"Since I was a cadet." Craig grinned. "My

dad was a Scot, very law abiding. He called them the polis."

"Don't you miss it after all that time?"

"A bit sometimes." He missed the feeling of being part of a team. But even that had been soured at the end. Anyway, what option had he had? "It was the right time to get out," he said.

"For you or them?" Gail asked.

"Both probably. My face didn't fit too well."

"I can imagine."

"What does that mean?"

"Well, the police are strong on discipline, aren't they? A bit like the Army, you have to conform. That doesn't strike me as your scene."

"It wasn't the discipline I minded," Craig said. "Ready?"

Although it was she who had suggested they play, Gail's mind no longer seemed to be on the game, and Craig soon went to 4–1. As he was retrieving a ball two planes flew over very low, following the line of the stream. The rasping roar of their engines shattered the quiet, and Craig waited for it to fade before serving.

"They come from the RAF station at Melsford," Gail told him.

He won the next two games and when he

asked if she wanted another set she shook her head.

"I'll go and root out Miles. He's neglected us long enough. Thanks for the game, Alan."

She walked away towards the wood and Craig headed for the house. Top of his list of priorities at the moment was a swim, and his trunks were in his room. As he passed the end of the house he saw that Gabriella too had gone now. The Laxtons were admiring the rose beds, but there was no sign of Caroline or Lorraine. Only the purr of the lawnmower in the distance broke the silence.

Then a woman screamed.

Distance diminished the sound, but couldn't purge it of its horror. Craig stopped, his hand on the handle of the French window. The scream had come from the direction of the wood, and he turned, dropping his racquet and the bag of balls, and started running across the lawn.

The Laxtons were standing near the pergola, apparently startled into immobility. As Craig passed they stared at him as if they had never seen him before. He ran on and met Fenn running towards the house. The writer was very pale.

"What's happened?" Craig demanded.

Fenn gasped for breath. "Somebody's shot Jordan."

Part of Craig's brain was surprised that he felt no sense of shock. Yet he couldn't have expected this.

"Is he alive?" he asked.

Fenn shook his head. "No." He gulped. "I'm going to phone the doctor and the police."

Craig let him go and walked on through the wood. It was blessedly cool under the trees, but he was hardly aware of it, he was thinking that in his experience when somebody was found shot the almost automatic assumption was that they had committed suicide. Perhaps it was an instinctive refusal to face up to the possibility of murder, or simply that suicide was more common. But Fenn had said categorically that somebody had shot Jordan. Why?

He emerged from the shadow of the trees on to the grassy terrace beside the river and saw three women near the summerhouse. Lorraine Maxwell had one arm round Caroline Rogers' shoulders and seemed to be trying to comfort her. Gail was standing a few feet away from them, her shoulders drooping. As Craig came up she looked at him, her eyes blank with shock, and her lips trembled. Not for the first time, it occurred to him that however accustomed people were to seeing violence on their television screens, it didn't prepare them for the reality.

He looked down at the grass. That dry, close-cropped turf would hold no traces of footprints, but all the same he said, "I think we'd better move away from here. The police won't want the ground trampled."

They went willingly enough, Caroline moving like an automaton, Lorraine's arm still round her. Then suddenly she wrenched herself free and, staring at the actress, said accusingly, "You killed him."

Lorraine regarded her calmly. "No, honey," she said.

"You did. I saw you. It's just like that other time." Caroline's voice, already pitched high with shock, rose higher.

Lorraine said nothing.

Leaving them, Craig walked up to the summerhouse and looked in. Jordan must have been typing on the little verandah, he was sitting at the old table Craig had seen that morning, his head slumped forward, his hands limp on the keyboard of an Adler portable.

Craig raised his head carefully. There was no doubt Jordan was dead, he had one neat bullet hole in his right temple and another just in front of his left ear. The edges were marked by a slight crust of dried blood. They were the sort of wounds a small calibre gun would make, Craig thought. Gently he lowered Jordan's head again and looked round. Apart from the essentials for his typing, a thin wad of A4 bond paper, a small plastic bottle of correcting fluid, some paper clips and a ballpoint pen, there was nothing on the table or the floor. The top sheet of paper was blank.

Going outside again Craig asked the three women, "Who found him?"

"I did," Lorraine answered, so quietly he hardly heard her.

"It was you screamed?"

"No."

"I did," Caroline said. She seemed to have herself under control now, and there was a sting of malice in her voice as she added, "She was standing there—just staring at him."

Craig had already noticed that none of the three was carrying a handbag, but even nowadays a woman, unless she was wearing a bikini or a skin-tight swimsuit, could conceal a small calibre pistol in her clothes. He would have liked to suggest they went away and searched each other now before the police came, it might well save a good deal of trouble and suspicion later, but he had no authority to do so and he suspected that Caroline Rogers, at least, would react furiously. Anyway, the case was nothing to do with him and the gun was probably in the river by now.

"Hallo."

Unnoticed by the little group, a woman of about thirty-three had approached along the bank. She was attractive with a rather round face and dark hair, but her eyes were hazel. She was wearing a white top and white cotton trousers and had a large black leather bag slung over her shoulder.

"Hallo," she said again in a pleasant, rather deep voice.

Caroline turned so quickly she nearly lost her balance and instinctively clutched at Lorraine Maxwell's arm. "Sandra! What the hell are you doing here?" Her voice was no longer pitched high, and now it was suddenly hard.

The newcomer looked annoyed, then she half laughed. "This is still my home, Caroline. Had you forgotten?" She studied their faces. "What's happened? Is something wrong?"

"You're Miles' wife?" Lorraine asked.

"Yes. I'm sorry, I'm afraid I don't . . ." Sandra Jordan eyed Lorraine more closely. "I know you, don't I? You're—"

"I'm Lorraine Maxwell," the actress said. "I'm sorry, there's been an accident."

"Accident?"

It was Craig who said gently, "I'm afraid Miles is dead."

"Oh God!" They watched helplessly while Sandra pulled herself together. "Where is he?"

"In the summerhouse," Craig answered. She made a move towards the little timber building and he added, "I shouldn't go in there."

Sandra stared at him. "Why not?"

"I'm sorry, it wasn't an accident, he was shot."

"*Shot*? You mean he . . . ?"

"We don't know what happened. Somebody's gone to call the police." Craig turned to the other women. "Don't you think it would be a good idea if you went up to the house with Mrs. Jordan? I'll wait here until the police come."

"That sounds sensible," Lorraine agreed.

71

The others said nothing, but they went willingly enough.

When they had gone Craig looked round. In a field just across the river a herd of cows was grazing placidly; fifty or sixty yards downstream an old rowing boat was nosed in to the bank, half-obscured by the trailing branches of an ash tree; somewhere in the wood behind him one of the pigeons which so angered Willy Davies coo-ed throatily.

It was an idyllic scene, but Craig's thoughts were less pleasant. He was reflecting that, although Jordan's hands had been resting on the typewriter keys when he was shot—unless someone had placed them there afterwards, and that seemed so unlikely it could almost be ruled out—there was no paper in the machine. Moreover the top sheet of the pile beside it was blank, and there was no sign of another with typing on it anywhere in the summerhouse. Which suggested that one sheet at least, possibly more, had been removed by somebody—most likely the murderer.

For Fenn had been right, Craig had no doubt about that, Jordan had been murdered. Not only was there no typing, there was no gun either.

Whatever he had planned for this weekend, it seemed fairly certain that it was connected in some way with the murder here thirty years ago. Three of his guests had been here then, and among the Randalls' other visitors was a man named Peter Fenn. So much Craig had learnt from his researches after Jordan's visit to his office. It looked as if Micky had been trying to recreate the Randalls' party.

But why? What was he up to? He had admitted there was something, and claimed it was only "a sort of game". Craig wondered if that was true. According to Jordan, his new television series would include programmes dealing with what he considered miscarriages of justice. Craig knew that old crimes, particularly murders, made popular television, and that sort of dramatic story, with an MP and a famous film star as two of the characters and more than a suggestion that the beautiful woman who was convicted was innocent, would have been meat and drink to Jordan. Moreover he would have handled it brilliantly.

But the evidence against Susan Randall had been overwhelming, if he was planning a programme like that he must have discovered something new. Was it possible that he had unearthed fresh evidence which suggested that one of the Randalls' guests had shot her husband, and that somebody here knew about it? Somebody who was frightened enough to murder him to prevent it being made public?

The bullets which killed him had been fired from a small calibre gun by somebody he knew well enough for him not to move when they approached him. And Willy Davies owned a ·22 rifle.

A siren wailed in the distance and Craig looked up. A police car was coming along the road from the village.

5

DETECTIVE CHIEF-SUPERINTEN-DENT ROBERT DESMOND GRANGER, the deputy head of the County CID, was a broad shouldered, barrel-chested, thick bellied man of fifty-five. He had a squarish head fringed with sandy hair going grey at the temples, a firm jaw and a short strong neck. Years ago he had acquired a reputation for being a hard man, difficult to please and demanding of his subordinates, and it had stuck to him. Men sometimes boasted they had worked under him—usually when they were no longer doing so.

In a way nowadays he used his reputation as a screen to hide behind, for much of his toughness had faded with his ambition, and now when he was hard to please it was due more to habit and the occasional peevishness of middle-age than a demand for more relentless work. The truth was that he was thinking more and more of retirement, the time until it came now counted in months rather than years. He didn't dodge work, he was too conscientious and had too much self-respect for that, but privately he hoped it wouldn't be too demanding. He knew, when he preached the paramount value of experience, that to some extent he was a hypocrite, and experience alone, without the will and ability to use it to the best advantage, couldn't better the hard driving force of ambition and comparative youth.

There had been a time when he almost enjoyed being called out in the middle of the night when a major case broke. No longer. And when he was away from his work he thought about it less and less. He was happily married with two children, a son at university and a daughter in her last year at school. Sometimes he worried about their futures. Especially Debbie's.

He regarded Craig now with an expression which was not so much cold as noncommittal. The others were up at the house, he would see what he could learn from this young fellow before he talked to them.

"Your name's Alan Craig?" he asked.

"Yes."

"You're staying here?"

"Just for the weekend."

It occurred to Granger that Craig didn't look the type to be a guest at this sort of party. Not that you could tell these days—and the dead man had worked in television.

"Has anything been touched here?" he asked.

"I don't know about the others," Craig said. "I moved his head to feel his pulse and make sure he was dead. I left him exactly as I found him."

"Are you a doctor?"

"No. I didn't need to be."

You're a cool young so-and-so, Granger thought. "Where were you when the shot was fired?" he asked.

"I don't know, I didn't hear it. I'd been playing tennis with Miss Lakeland, it was hot and I was on my way to my room to fetch my things for a swim when I heard a woman scream."

"Who told you what had happened?"

"I came to see what was up. I met Simon Fenn coming back to the house to call your people, and he told me."

He's got it all worked out, Granger told himself, his irritation mounting. Yet he had to admit Craig didn't seem the usual sort of smart alec. Nor, apparently, was he taking any pleasure in relating what he knew, he was sticking to a calm, straightforward recital of the facts.

"Did you notice the time when you heard the scream?" he enquired, half hoping to catch the younger man out.

"Yes, it was eighteen minutes to four."

"You're sure about that?"

"Yes, I looked at my watch."

"Why? You didn't suspect what had happened, did you?"

Why had he? Craig wondered. Had he, subconsciously, suspected something of the sort?

"No, of course not," he said.

"Do you know who it was screamed?"

"Mrs. Rogers, I think."

"So she found the body?"

"No, that was Miss Maxwell."

Granger referred to a list. "They were here when you arrived?"

"Yes."

"Was anybody else with them?"

"Miss Lakeland. Mrs. Jordan came along a few minutes later."

Granger looked at his notes again, checking that the names were on the list the uniformed sergeant who had been first on the scene had prepared.

"You came straight here from the house?" he asked.

"Yes."

"Did you see anybody apart from Mr. Fenn on the way?"

"The Laxtons. They were looking at the roses."

Granger nodded. "Thank you, Mr. Craig. I'd like another word with you later."

Craig returned the nod and started walking back through the wood to the house. Granger wasn't at all like his old guv'nor in appearance or manner, he told himself, so why did he feel this instinctive antipathy towards him?

There was no one on the verandah, and when he entered the drawing-room he found the rest of the party with the exception of Caroline Rogers gathered there. Caroline, it seemed, had gone to her room to lie down.

When Craig came in there was a sudden awkward silence. He knew they had been talking about him, probably reminding each other he had been a policeman and wondering what attitude they should adopt towards him. Did they realise yet that almost certainly whoever shot Jordan was here in the house? Probably in this room?

Sandra looked strained and somehow lonely, he thought. Then he remembered that very likely Caroline was the only one of the guests she had met before this afternoon. She had told the older woman that this was her home, yet now she was virtually a stranger here. What had her relationship with Jordan been?

It was Fenn who broke the silence. "Where are they?" he demanded. "What are they doing?"

"Going over the summerhouse, I think," Craig replied.

"Don't you know?"

"Why should I? They haven't taken me into their confidence."

"You're one of them, aren't you?"

"No, I'm not." Craig was nettled.

"They'll want to talk to all of us," Laxton observed reasonably. "They're bound to. You should go and lie down, Mrs. Jordan."

Sandra gave him a wan smile. "I'd rather be here," she said. "It's all so horrible, I don't want to be alone."

"Of course not," Elizabeth Laxton agreed with a warmth which surprised Craig. Then she glanced across to where Gabriella Fenn was sitting and her expression hardened.

The author's wife had been weeping, and she dabbed at her eyes repeatedly with a tiny handkerchief. It occurred to Craig that she was revelling in the display of her grief, and he wondered if she hoped to upstage Gail, who looked shocked and pale but had her feelings under control. Was Gabriella proclaiming that her love for Jordan had been stronger than the blonde girl's? Or, perhaps, that because of it she couldn't possibly have killed him? If so, she was not only a poor psychologist, but also both cleverer and more subtle than she seemed.

"For heaven's sake don't make so much fuss," Fenn muttered.

"You do not understand," Gabriella moaned. "Nobody can understand."

Judging by the writer's expression, Craig thought, he understood only too well. Was Gabriella protesting too much or merely indulging in a fit of Latin temperament?

"The police will want to know where we all were when Jordan was shot," he remarked. The others regarded him with looks that varied from uneasiness in the case of Caroline to outright

81

hostility from Laxton. "Did anybody hear the shot?"

"I didn't," Gail said.

"Nor did I." Gabriella sniffed. "If I 'ad . . ."

It wasn't clear what she would have done, nor what difference it would have made, and nobody asked her.

"You have no right to question us," Laxton complained loudly.

"He has a *right*," Elizabeth corrected him. "Although it's hardly one most people would care to exercise."

Craig resolved not to let his anger show. "I'm not questioning you," he said. "I simply wondered if anybody heard the shot because I didn't and it could be important. It's up to you —but I can't see what harm it can do."

It seemed that nobody had heard it. Which was strange, Craig thought, because even a ·22 gun made enough noise when it was fired for those of them on the lawn at least to have heard it. Then he understood. Those planes! The shot must have been fired while they were flying over.

"You were the first to get to the summer-house," he observed to Lorraine.

The actress met his eyes calmly. "After whoever shot Miles," she agreed. "I guess so."

"But it wasn't you who screamed."

"No, that was Caroline. She came along and found me standing there and she must have thought I . . ."

"Then Simon arrived."

"I'd been with Gabriella," Fenn said.

"No, Simon, not then. You were angry because of Miles and me and you walked off. I saw you going towards the garage. Don't you remember?"

Fenn gave his wife a venomous look. "That was afterwards," he said.

"Oh no, it was before." For the first time since Craig came into the room Gabriella smiled. It wasn't a pleasant smile.

However it wasn't Craig's job to encourage the Fenns to quarrel in the hope that more indiscretions would come tumbling out, and the talk was drifting away from the point he was trying to establish.

"How long was it before Caroline came along?" he asked Lorraine.

The actress thought for a moment. "Time seems to go so slowly when a thing like that happens," she observed. Then, as if realizing the implication of what she had said, she added, "I guess it was about twenty seconds. Maybe not that long."

Caroline had found her staring down at Jordan's body just as, thirty years ago, she had found Susan Randall gazing at her husband's. It must have seemed that history was repeating itself bizarrely; no wonder she had screamed. Her screams had brought Fenn and, a minute or two later, Craig himself. If he was right and the shot had been fired while the two planes were flying over, that put it within a few minutes either way of 3.30. The police could hardly hope to pinpoint it more accurately than that—unless the RAF people could say exactly when the planes were overhead.

"Mr. Craig," Elizabeth said, "why did Miles Jordan invite you here this weekend?"

"Elizabeth!" Lorraine protested.

But Craig knew they were all watching him, wondering the same thing. "I don't know," he answered.

"You expect us to believe that?" Fenn demanded sarcastically.

"I don't care whether you believe it or not. I asked him two or three times; he wouldn't tell me."

"Why pick on Alan?" Gail asked.

"Because he's the only one who . . ." Laxton stopped.

"Who what?"

Who isn't one of us, Craig thought. But he was wrong.

"Who hasn't any connection with what happened here before."

"That's what it's all about, isn't it?" Fenn's voice rose.

"I'm not the only one, you're forgetting Gail and the Fenns," Craig pointed out, glancing at the girl. The others looked too, and she bit her lip.

"There was a Fenn here then," Laxton said.

"He was my father." Fenn spoke more calmly now. "My mother was here too. They weren't married then; her name was Jane Marsh."

"Jane Marsh is your mother?" Laxton looked as if he found it difficult to believe.

"Yes."

"Oh Jesus!" Lorraine breathed. "I guess that leaves you and Alan, honey."

"My father's a doctor," Gail said very quietly. "My mother died years ago. Look, I don't know what all this is about."

"So why did Miles ask you here?" Gabriella demanded.

"At least we know that," her husband told her vindictively.

The others looked embarrassed.

"What was your mother's maiden name?" Laxton asked.

Gail hesitated. "Why? What's it got to do with what's happened?"

"Nothing," Lorraine told her.

"It was James. Alison James."

Lorraine looked at Laxton. "What happened to Mary and Roger?"

"Roger died of leukaemia. It must be twenty years ago. He never married."

"And Mary Whittaker?"

"I don't know," Laxton said abruptly. It was obvious that he was lying.

"Which brings us back to you," Fenn told Craig.

"It's clear Miles was planning something for that dreadful programme of his," Elizabeth said. "I suppose it was something to do with what happened here before."

There was an uneasy silence.

"Did he tell you anything?" Craig asked Gail.

"No. I'd hardly seen him lately." The girl

glanced across at Sandra, then away again, blushing faintly. "I know he was looking forward to this weekend though."

"He phoned me the other day," Sandra said. "He told me he was having some people down. That was all."

"He did not tell me anything either," Gabriella added.

Nobody took any notice.

A uniformed constable appeared in the doorway, looked round at them and finally focussed on Craig. "Mr. Craig, sir? Chief Superintendent Granger would like to have another word with you please, sir."

Craig stood up. "Where is he?" he asked.

"In the room on the right at the end of the hall, sir."

The others watched in silence as the constable stood aside for Craig to go out first.

6

"**Y**OU'RE a private detective," Granger said, a slight but nonetheless mildly offensive emphasis on the last two words. "I suppose you think you know it all?"

So he's one of those, Craig thought, determined not to allow himself to be riled. "Yes," he said. "And no. In that order."

"I don't like private detectives. Most of the ones I've known have been ex-coppers who weren't any good in the Force. They weren't much damn good as private detectives either. How long have you been one?"

"A few weeks."

"And before that?"

"A detective-sergeant—in the Met."

Granger digested the information and a hard look came into his eyes. "The Met eh? You're what—thirty-three? Thirty-four?"

"Thirty-four."

"Did you jack it in or did they throw you out?"

Craig let five seconds elapse, then he asked, "Has that anything to do with this inquiry?"

"I don't know. It may not have—or it may have a lot. Have you anything to hide?"

"No."

"If that's true, you could be a help to us. You're a trained observer, you were on the spot and you knew what to look for."

"Don't try and involve me," Craig said. "I'm just a guest here like the others."

"Not like the others—you used to be a copper," Granger told him.

"That's right, used to be. I'm not any longer." Craig paused. "And I've had superintendents up to here."

Only a slight heightening of his colour showed that Granger had heard. "They must have wept tears of blood when they lost you," he said.

Craig grinned. "I'll tell you all I know about what happened this afternoon, but don't expect me to be working for you."

"You're loyal to your friends?"

"They aren't my friends; I'd never met any of them until I got here yesterday."

"So tell me," Granger said harshly, nodding

at the constable in the corner to indicate he should start taking notes.

They were in the library. Jordan's body had been photographed from every possible angle, examined by the divisional police surgeon and removed to the mortuary for the post mortem. The summerhouse had been examined and now every surface which might be capable of retaining traces was being fingerprinted. Men were searching every inch of the ground round it, while others were combing the wood and the bank of the river. With the routine of the system established and under way Granger had decided to see Craig again before any of the others in the hope that he might have noticed something they hadn't. Detective-Inspector Franklin had been dispatched to interview Davies and his wife.

"Do you know what killed him?" Craig asked.

Granger looked as if he was about to point out forcibly that he was the one asking the questions, then changed his mind. "Two shots from a small calibre gun, probably a two-two," he answered.

"There's a two-two rifle here," Craig told him.

"Where?"

"Davies, the gardener, has one. He was out with it this morning."

"What do you mean, out with it?"

"He was shooting pigeons."

Granger thought for a moment, but let it go at that. "How long had you known Miles Jordan?" he asked.

"About twenty years. We were at school together." Craig saw the flicker of disbelief in the older man's eyes. "Lancaster Grove Comprehensive. Did you think he went to Eton?"

"Don't worry about what I think."

"We hadn't seen each other since I left until a few weeks ago."

"What happened then?"

"I got an envelope in the post. There was nothing in it except a copy of a newspaper report of a murder trial in 1954."

"Go on." Granger had been listening before, now his interest showed.

"The defendant was a woman named Susan Randall; she was accused of shooting her husband. The jury found her guilty." There was a momentary pause, then Craig went on, "The next day I got an invitation for this

91

weekend. I couldn't think why Miles Jordan should ask me, I didn't know him and it wasn't my scene. Then he came to see me and reminded me about us being at school together. His name was Michael then. I asked him why he wanted me to come, but all he'd say was that he did. He was very insistent. I said it had something to do with the cutting, didn't it, and he admitted he'd sent it but not why. Just that he thought I'd be interested in it. I didn't know his house was where Randall was murdered."

"Why do you think he sent you the report?" Granger enquired.

"To get me interested."

"That all?"

Again Craig hesitated. "I think he had some idea of using the case in one of his programmes," he said.

"Are you saying you think there's some connection between the two murders?" Granger asked. The barely concealed hostility was less evident now, he was experienced and shrewd enough to realise that if Craig knew anything antagonising him wasn't the best way to find out what it was.

"There could be," Craig replied.

"Two of the people who are staying here now were here then?"

"Three. Lorraine Maxwell, Charles Laxton and Caroline Rogers—she was Caroline Bateman then. And Fenn's parents were here too."

The Superintendent's expression didn't change but he muttered something under his breath. He was reflecting that everything pointed to this being a complicated case and one which would attract a lot of attention. That could hardly be avoided when the victim was a television celebrity as well-known as Jordan, and two of his guests a film star and an MP. Granger could do without complications and the attention of the media. If he had to be landed with another murder before he retired, why couldn't it have been a nice simple straightforward domestic, not this theatrical set-up. Ye gods! A thirty year old murder, half the people who had been here then here now, the host shot in almost a carbon copy of the earlier crime; it was too much.

"I was a d/c then," he remarked, reminiscence mellowing him. "Old Tom Levine was in charge. We called him Basher, he came from up in Suffolk somewhere. Swede basher. He's still alive, must be over eighty now."

"Was there any doubt about Susan Randall being guilty?" Craig asked. That, it seemed to him, must be the crux of the whole business, nothing less than a miscarriage of justice with the victim dying in prison would have interested Jordan. Tragedy wasn't enough, there had to be an element of something else, the oppression of the helpless innocent by the merciless Law. Perhaps a suggestion of incompetence or wilful blindness on the part of the police or the defence.

"None," Granger said with certainty. "You say you read the report."

It was what Craig had expected. And yet . . . Was it possible Jordan had discovered something?

"Thirty years ago," he said, "the Batemans found her standing looking at her husband's body with the gun that killed him on the floor by her feet. This time Caroline found Lorraine Maxwell looking at Jordan—but there was no gun. That's the difference."

"It's too damned stagey," Granger said disgustedly.

"Maybe that was deliberate."

"What do you mean?"

"I don't know exactly," Craig admitted. It was just a vague idea which had come into his head a moment ago, but there were at least two people in the house who had a professional interest in theatrical effects—Lorraine and Fenn.

"All right," Granger said. He was anxious to get back from the shifting sands of Craig's theorising to the firm ground of his familiar routine. "Tell me what you did this afternoon."

Craig obeyed.

When he had finished and answered a few questions the Superintendent asked, "Is there anything else you can tell me?" Craig shook his head. "That's all for the time being then. You aren't thinking of leaving here, are you?"

"No," Craig answered. He wasn't.

He went out. But he didn't return to the drawing-room, he wanted to be alone to think about the ideas that were jumbling his brain. Going out to the verandah, he carried a deck chair to a sunny corner where he was unlikely to be disturbed, and settled down.

Everything seemed to point to Jordan's death having some connection with Randall's murder all those years ago, and the only people who had been here then were Lorraine, Caroline and Laxton. That narrowed the field.

One thing about the guests especially interested Craig, none of them appeared to have known Jordan long. Lorraine Maxwell said she had met him for the first time a few weeks ago in New York; Gail, according to her, had known him three months. Craig had gained the impression that neither the Laxtons nor Caroline were old acquaintances, and Fenn had worked on only two of Jordan's latest programmes.

Looked at in that light there seemed something contrived about this party. Had Jordan set out to get to know as many of the people who had been the Randalls' guests all those years ago as he could? And because he couldn't get in touch with two of them he had substituted their son? It was almost inconceivable, but if he had been planning a programme about the Randall case, with a team of researchers at his disposal tracing them probably wouldn't have been too difficult.

But why all the secrecy and pretence? Because he had known that if his prospective guests discovered what he was planning they would take fright like startled deer? Laxton, for one, would hardly relish having his involvement in an almost forgotten murder brought to light, however innocent it was. The same applied to his wife, Elizabeth's devotion to his career and his public position was obvious. Lorraine, too, would probably prefer old scandals to remain buried. Divorce, even in triplicate, a Hollywood star could survive without losing her fans, a sordid murder might be a different matter.

But why bring them all here? What had Micky been planning?

Craig was glad the case wasn't his responsibility, he didn't envy Granger.

He heard footsteps coming along the verandah towards him and, looking round, saw Elizabeth Laxton carrying another deck chair.

"Don't get up," she told him as he made a move to do so. Setting up the chair beside his, but not too close to it, she sat down. "Mr. Craig, Miles Jordan said you were some kind of detective." She was careful to remove any trace of disapproval from her voice. "What experience have you had?"

Craig wasn't sure whether he should be angered or amused; it wouldn't have occurred to the MP's wife that she might seem offensive.

"The usual," he answered laconically. "I've

97

been shot at once or twice, assaulted, seen a friend shot dead by a nutter the doctors let out because they said he was cured, assisted on I don't know how many murder investigations and robberies. Not to mention muggings and rape. I used to be a detective-sergeant in the Met."

"And now?" Elizabeth Laxton enquired coolly. If Craig had intended his recital to shock her he had failed. "You're working for yourself?"

"Yes." Ironically, he added, "I haven't peeped through a keyhole since I left the police."

Suddenly Elizabeth laughed. It was a genuinely amused sound and Craig, surprised, grinned back.

"It wasn't idle curiosity," she assured him. "Will you do a job for me?"

"That depends what it is." She was continually surprising him, he thought. Which was odd for such a predictable woman.

"I want to know what Miles Jordan was up to."

She wasn't alone in wanting to know that, Craig reflected. But if she was prepared to pay him to find out, that was all right with him.

"You think he was up to something?" he asked.

"Of course he was. You know that as well as I do. He admitted it this morning."

Craig had been thinking that himself a few minutes ago. When Lorraine tried to assure Fenn Jordan wasn't planning anything, he had contradicted her, "Oh but I am." Perhaps, figuratively speaking, he had signed his own death warrant with those four words.

There was something else he remembered: Elizabeth saying that men like Jordan were dangerous.

"Excuse me asking," he said, "but you didn't kill him, did you?"

For a moment she looked angry, then her stern features relaxed and she answered simply, "No, I didn't. But I would hardly tell you if I did, would I?"

"No," Craig agreed, "but you might give yourself away when you said it. And I had to ask."

"Why?"

Craig grinned again. "To satisfy my conscience."

With delicate irony Mrs. Laxton said, "Oh, I see. Will you take the job?"

"Yes. But you have to understand, if I learn anything the police should know, I shall have to tell them. This isn't America, we don't have their privileges. Or is that only in books?"

"I've no idea," Elizabeth told him. "Very well, I accept that."

"Okay. As you're here, I may as well begin by asking you some questions. Like what do you know about the first murder? The one in 1954?"

"Practically nothing. As far as I can remember, my husband never mentioned it to me until this weekend, and I don't recall reading anything about it at the time, although I suppose I must have done." An edge to her tone, Elizabeth Laxton added, "They weren't the sort of people I knew."

Craig resisted the temptation to point out that she had married one of them. "You hadn't met any of the people staying here before this weekend?" he asked.

"To the best of my knowledge and belief no, but because of Charles' position I meet a great many people and I certainly don't remember half of them afterwards." She paused. "You think the two—crimes are connected?"

"It seems on the cards," Craig replied.

100

"It's all very unpleasant."

"Murder usually is. Especially for the person who gets murdered."

Elizabeth looked as if she considered that remark in extremely bad taste. "I have never had anything to do with anything like this before," she said. Unexpectedly she added, "Miles Jordan was a common little man and malicious. One can't have people like him endangering everything worthwhile." She stood up.

7

FOR a while after Elizabeth Laxton left him Craig didn't move. He didn't think that her last bitter observation about Jordan meant anything, except that she had disliked him and all he stood for; she wasn't naïve enough to reveal her feelings if it mattered. And he doubted if she would have tried a double bluff for the simple reason that she wouldn't credit him with the intelligence to give it any point. That was the blind spot of people like Laxton's wife, their unconscious arrogance led them to underrate those they regarded as their social inferiors.

He knew his position vis-à-vis the police was delicate, to say the least. While he had every right to take on the job she had offered him, Granger was hardly likely to welcome his making his own inquiries. Well, that was just too bad.

Craig found Sandra alone in the kitchen.

"I thought we could all do with a cup of tea,"

she explained. "And I wanted something to do."

He thought she was taking what had happened surprisingly coolly. Then he saw the strained look about her eyes and her hands trembling slightly as she took a large teapot out of a cupboard and he changed his mind. Sandra, apparently, was not a woman who revealed her feelings to everybody.

"My name's Alan Craig," he said.

"I know. Caroline told me."

"You knew her before today."

"We'd met. Miles invited her to a party in London just before we split up. She didn't know anybody else there so we talked a lot of the time." Sandra turned, still holding the teapot. "She said you were a detective. Is that true?"

"Yes. What else did she say?"

"Nothing much really. She was too upset." Sandra turned back to the table and spooned tea into the pot. "What sort of detective are you?"

"I used to be in the police, now I work for myself."

"Does that mean you follow errant wives to see what they get up to?"

Craig guessed that Sandra's brightness was forced and that behind it she was more shocked than she was prepared for him to see. "Or husbands?"

"Are there such things as errant wives these days?"

"Oh yes. But Miles didn't need a detective, we were honest with each other. I was with him, anyway. So why did he ask you here?" Sandra returned the tea caddy to the cupboard. "I'm sorry, I didn't mean that to sound rude. You just don't seem his type."

"I don't know why," Craig told her. "He said it hadn't anything to do with my work." But had he said quite that? Craig couldn't remember.

"That doesn't mean anything. When he wanted to get his own way he could lie like a . . ." Sandra stopped. "A trooper swears and a lord gets drunk, who is it lies?"

"I don't know."

"He could convince himself. Like politicians do."

With them the ability was an essential qualification, Craig thought, but there were plenty of other people who possessed it—and not all of them knew. Had Micky been one of them?

The kettle had begun to boil. Sandra switched it off and poured water into the teapot. It occurred to Craig that there was something unreal about their being here calmly discussing her husband only two or three hours after he had been murdered, while she made tea. But then, the whole business was unreal. Micky had made sure of that.

"Did you know any of the others before this afternoon?" he asked.

"No. Only by name." Sandra busied herself getting out crockery and spoons. "Even in the old days I didn't know a lot of the people Miles met through his work, and lately I haven't met any of them. I stay down here and he's in town most of the time."

"It's a lovely house," Craig observed. "How long have you had it?"

"About six months, we moved at the end of January. Miles' uncle died last year and left him some money, he saw this house when he was driving past one day and set his heart on living here. He made inquiries to find out who owned it and if they'd be prepared to sell and, as it happened, they were getting on and finding it too big for them and they were glad to. He didn't tell me anything about it until it was all settled, then he just announced one day we were moving here. I was furious. Not about the house, I loved it as soon as I saw it, just the way he did it."

Craig wondered which had come first, seeing the house or Jordan's interest in the Randall case. He was inclined to think the latter. For one thing, you could hardly see the house from the road, it was almost hidden by the rhododendrons and the corner of the wood. Had Micky come down to see where the Randalls had lived, and decided on the spur of the moment to buy it?

He couldn't have been planning this weekend even then, could he?

"Do you live here?" Craig asked. Seeing Sandra's quizzical look, he added, "I'm sorry, it's none of my business."

"There's no secret about it, you ask anybody in the village and they'll tell you. The answer's yes and no, I'm here part of the time, when Miles is—was in London." Sandra's voice dropped, as if she was shocked by the implications of the past tense. Then she went on, "It was all very civilised, we didn't fight or anything. We were still good friends."

"You said you knew he was having a party this weekend."

"Yes. We used to warn each other to save embarrassment; it would have been awkward if he'd brought one of his girl friends down and found me in residence." Sandra gave Craig a level look. "Now I suppose you're going to ask me where I live when I'm not here?"

"No," he said.

"Good, that really would be none of your business. Do you want to know why I came here this afternoon?"

"If you want to tell me."

"You may as well know. There were some business things I had to discuss with Miles. I didn't want to run into any of his guests if I could help it, so I asked Mrs. Davies where he was. She told me in the summerhouse, and I went straight there."

By the path which skirted the side of the lawn, Craig supposed.

"When Micky told you about having some people here, did he say anything about them?" he asked.

"No, I'm sure he didn't."

"He was planning something."

"Miles was always planning something," Sandra responded with a touch of bitterness.

"Had you seen him lately?"

"You're asking a lot of questions." She began piling crockery on a tray. "Is it just curiosity or are you working?"

"Both," Craig answered. "I was one of the people he invited and I'd like to know why. We hadn't seen each other for nearly twenty years and, you said yourself, I'm not his type."

"That was intended to be a compliment." Sandra picked up the tray and Craig opened the door for her. "Thank you." Level with him she paused. "I suppose I seem very hard and unfeeling to you, don't I?"

Craig thought there was something rather touching, a hint of vulnerability, in the question, and he said awkwardly, "Shock takes people different ways."

"Yes," Sandra agreed.

It was only later Craig remembered she hadn't answered his question about when she had last seen Micky. Was it because something had happened then that she didn't want him to know? He wondered if she had told Granger.

Craig wanted to talk to Lorraine, she had been

here when Randall was shot and from seemingly casual observations she had made he believed she knew—or, at least, suspected—more than anyone else about this weekend. But when he returned to the drawing-room with Sandra the actress wasn't there and he gathered Granger had summoned her to the library.

Elizabeth Laxton, her back no longer quite so straight and her head drooping slightly, was sitting in one of the big easy chairs looking tired. Beside her, her husband fidgeted restlessly with the arms of his chair.

Gail was making a pretence of reading a magazine but she wasn't taking in what she saw. When Sandra and Craig entered the room she looked up, then quickly away again. Hers must be a pretty embarrassing position now with Sandra here, Craig thought.

Apparently Caroline hadn't reappeared, and when he asked where the Fenns were Laxton grunted something about their having gone out to the garden. From his tone Craig understood he had been glad to see the back of them. He didn't blame him, the combination of Gabriella's boasting and tears and her husband's outbursts had been trying before, it was doubly so now. All the same, he stepped out on to the verandah and stood there for a few seconds listening. Hearing nothing, he walked towards the corner of the house to his right. He had nearly reached it when he heard Fenn say spitefully, "How do I know you didn't kill him? You were in the wood."

"Why should I kill 'im?" Gabriella demanded, not bothering to lower her voice, which was penetrating at any time. "'E loved me."

"He never loved you," Fenn told her violently. "He never loved anyone except himself. Can't you understand that?"

There was a moment's silence, then Gabriella demanded, "Where are you going?"

"Anywhere where I don't have to listen to your bleating about how Jordan loved you," Fenn replied. "I'm glad he's dead."

Craig waited for ten seconds or so, then he rounded the corner of the house. The author was stalking away in the direction of the beech hedge and Gabriella, looking angry but not in the least distressed, was gazing after him. It was so like a scene from a bad 1930's play Craig felt like laughing, but he supposed it was real enough to them.

"Are you alone?" he enquired cheerfully.

Gabriella turned an unfriendly eye on him. "Yes."

Craig decided subtleties would be wasted on her and he was more likely to achieve results using shock tactics. "You think Simon shot Jordan?" he asked.

The unfriendly look became a sullen stare. "He did not kill Miles," Gabriella declared. "He 'ad plenty of reason to, but 'e didn't." As if it were an afterthought she added contemptuously, "He wouldn't 'ave 'ad the courage."

She sounded very sure, Craig thought, and he wondered if she knew something or was merely defending her husband. After all, if there were no direct link between the two murders Fenn had as strong a motive as anyone for shooting Jordan.

"Who did then?" he asked.

"'Ow should I know?"

"I just thought you seemed to know something." There was an unpleasant, cunning look in Gabriella's eyes, Craig thought. Rather abruptly he added, "If you do, you'd better tell the police. You're asking for trouble if you don't."

Turning, he walked back to the front of the house. Despite her denial, he was pretty sure she knew something—or thought she did. Whether it was anything important was a different matter. He wondered why Elizabeth Laxton wanted him to find out what Jordan had planned instead of leaving it to the police. What was she afraid of?

When Craig left the room Gail watched him go uncertainly. What was he doing here? She could account for the others, they were the sort of people Miles would know, but Craig was different. She couldn't help wondering if they had really been old friends and, if so, if that was the only reason Miles had invited him. She was beginning to understand that Jordan had rarely done anything without a good reason.

At first he had seemed charming and attentive. Affectionate, too. But lately she had realised his was a complex personality, difficult, perhaps impossible for her to understand. There had been times when it was as if she had glimpsed another side of him, a dark side he kept hidden from the world. It made her uneasy, almost afraid.

Now she had a new, more urgent fear. The police would check up on everybody here, probing into their lives and revealing their secrets. If they discovered the truth it would all have been in vain.

She wished there was somebody here she could talk to, but she had nothing in common with the Laxtons and, even if she hadn't rather disliked her, Caroline was too absorbed in herself. Confiding to Gabriella or her husband was out of the question. She could have talked to Lorraine, she thought, but the actress was closeted with Granger.

Sandra's arrival on the scene had made things worse. Why had she come when she knew Miles was having a party this weekend? Gail reflected that she had expected to dislike Sandra if they met, now they had she didn't. She wondered if Miles' wife hated her.

The Laxtons were murmuring to each other, taking no notice of anyone else. Gail put down her magazine and walked out to the hall, then out by the front door, almost colliding with Craig who was coming in.

"I wanted a breath of fresh air," she explained. "I couldn't stand it in there any longer. Will we have to stay here long?"

"That depends on the police," Craig answered.

"I thought you might know."

"Why? I'm nothing to do with them."

Gail wondered if she could believe him. There had been something reassuring, yet at the same time slightly alarming, about the way he had taken charge this afternoon. It was as if, from being an observer, he had suddenly revealed himself as what he had really been all along, one of the leading characters in the drama. She started walking along the verandah and was pleased when he went with her.

"You're taking it well," he remarked.

She eyed him uncertainly, not sure whether what he said had contained an implied criticism.

"It doesn't seem real somehow. I still can't quite believe it's happened. And I can't feel shattered. I suppose I should, but I don't even feel terribly sad. I was going to tell Miles this weekend that I didn't want to go on." Craig said nothing. "He wasn't like I thought he was at first. He was cruel sometimes. He enjoyed it, that was the worst. Have you seen his programmes when he's tricked somebody into appearing and then got them in a corner? He used to say he was Society's vengeance and I know they were mostly crooks but . . . He had to dominate people. He'd be charming and wheedle them into doing what he wanted, then he'd drop them."

Craig remembered Micky at school. Even then he had possessed a gift for making people do what he wanted.

"You said he was looking forward to this weekend," he reminded Gail.

"He seemed sort of excited. Keyed up. Like a little boy looking forward to a special treat." She paused. "Do you think Elizabeth was right and he was planning to do a programme about that other murder?"

"It could be. But I can't see what. There doesn't seem any doubt Susan Randall shot her husband."

"Miles wouldn't have wasted time on something unless he knew he could make a success of it," Gail said. "He was the most professional person I've ever known, and he always had a reason for what he was doing. Most people haven't half the time, but he was different. I suppose that's why he was so successful."

They had walked part of the way along the path skirting the lawn and for a few moments neither of them spoke. Then Craig asked, "Had he been having an affair with Gabriella?"

"Yes. That's how he met Simon. Why?"

"I think he had an obsession."

"What do you mean? What obsession?"

"I don't know. Something to do with the Randall business."

"Will the police find who killed him?" There was an undertone of fear in Gail's voice.

"I expect so. They nearly always do."

The girl looked up at the sky. A mass of pewter coloured cloud loomed menacingly to the south-west, and even as she looked there was a low rumble of thunder.

"There's going to be a storm," she said. "I hate them."

They turned and headed back towards the house. As they reached the verandah heavy spots of rain pattered on the gravel behind them. Lightning flashed and this time the thunder was much closer.

They were crossing the hall when the library door opened and Lorraine came out looking distressed. Seeing them she smiled faintly and started up the stairs. Granger followed her out of the room, saw Gail and Craig and stopped.

"Davies's gun is missing," he said.

8

NOBODY was very interested in eating that evening. Mrs. Davies had prepared a cold supper but most of the guests only toyed with their food. It occurred to Craig that somebody should write a treatise on the relationship between shock and appetite, but probably they already had. However, while they didn't eat much, Laxton and Fenn both drank a good deal, and by the end of the meal the former's thin cheeks were flushed and the author's manner had become increasingly morose.

Sandra, the signs of strain more apparent now, had tacitly assumed the role of hostess. Craig guessed Gail had been only too glad to relinquish it.

Caroline Rogers had reappeared just before they went into the dining room, wearing too much make-up inexpertly applied, but showing no other signs of distress. Not for the first time, Craig suspected that her slightly fluffy manner was misleading and that she was a good deal tougher than she liked people to see. He had met women like her while he was in the Force, implacable women who would fight relentlessly for what they considered theirs, and not be over-scrupulous about the weapons they used.

All of them round the table were uncomfortably aware of the police in the house. The knowledge inhibited them so that, despite one or two attempts by Lorraine supported by Elizabeth Laxton to behave as if nothing untoward had happened, it was a subdued and almost silent meal. Even Lorraine looked worried and lacked her usual sparkle. Craig wondered if his presence was affecting them too, several of them obviously still regarded him as a police spy.

The disappearance of Willie Davies's rifle suggested it had been used to shoot Jordan, he reflected. If the gardener or his wife were guilty, then almost certainly the murder had nothing to do with Randall's death, and Craig couldn't believe that. Too many things pointed to a link. But to rule out the Davieses almost certainly meant the murderer was here in this room. He looked round the table. With the exception of Lorraine's—and Gail's, too, he thought—they were such ordinary faces. Not that that meant anything, the most vicious killers were often the most ordinary looking people.

Only Caroline, Lorraine and Laxton had been here when Randall was shot, had Jordan known something about one of them which had driven that person to murder him?

At last the meal came to an end and they began drifting rather aimlessly away. Craig saw Caroline go out on to the verandah. She hesitated there for a second or two, looking both ways, before turning and setting off in the direction of the tennis court. He waited until she reached the corner of the house, then he followed her.

The storm had passed, and it was a fine, clear evening with the raindrops on the lawn sparkling in the last of the sunlight and the wood darkly shadowed against the sky. The air was still pleasantly warm, and it seemed to Craig it smelt cleaner and fresher.

When she was halfway to the tennis court Caroline stopped. Craig knew she must have heard him behind her, but she didn't turn to see who it was.

"It's better now the storm's gone," he volunteered, coming up to her.

She gave an affected, humourless little laugh. "I'm glad you think so." Her voice, rather high-pitched and empty, somehow made nearly everything she said seem meaningless.

It grated on Craig. "The weather I meant," he explained.

"Oh. Yes, I suppose so. I hadn't noticed." Caroline started to walk on. She had bad feet and she walked slowly, as if every step was painful.

Craig matched his pace to hers. "You said you were here when Nigel Randall was shot, didn't you?" he asked.

"What's that got to do with it?" Caroline demanded.

I've alarmed her, Craig thought. Frightened, she would probably clam up and he would learn nothing. Aloud he said, "Nothing, has it?"

She gave him a quick sideways look. "No. How could it have?"

"All the same, it's strange Micky invited three people here this weekend who were here then."

"I don't know anything about it. I hadn't seen him for weeks."

"It makes it seem as if there must be some connection."

Caroline stopped and stared at him. "What do you mean?" she demanded.

"I'm not sure yet." There was no doubt she was frightened, Craig told himself, the question was, what had frightened her and when? Was it something Jordan knew or his death? The answer to that might throw light on a lot of things. "Do you think Susan Randall killed her husband?" he asked.

Caroline started forward again. "Of course she did. Everybody knew that."

"You never had any doubt?"

"No. She was jealous and possessive and Nigel was a very attractive man. She had plenty of motive."

Craig didn't care for the malice in Caroline's voice, although he thought he knew the reason for it. "It must have been a nasty experience for you, finding him and having to give evidence," he said.

"It was horrible," Caroline agreed, shuddering. "And this afternoon brought it all back. It was ghastly."

"You liked Randall?"

Again she gave Craig a sideways glance. "Did somebody say I did?"

"No. But you said he was attractive, and it's

obvious you felt what happened very much."
Privately Craig doubted if Caroline felt anything
very much unless it affected her own wellbeing.
He was pretty sure she had stayed in her room
this afternoon not because she was distressed
but to avoid questions she was reluctant to
answer.

"We had been rather close," she admitted
now with a blend of wariness and self-satisfac-
tion Craig found extremely distasteful. "But it
was all over before then. Not that there was
ever anything . . . Rupert, my first husband,
knew all about it."

"Why did you come this weekend?" Craig
asked. "Back to the house where it happened?"

"Miles tricked me. He said it would be an
amusing weekend with some interesting people.
I thought he meant people from television.
Stars. I'd never have come if I'd known it was
the same house and he . . ."

Craig was ready to believe her. "Where were
you when he was shot?" he asked casually. Her
face seemed to tighten and he added, "I'm
sorry, I was just curious where we all were. I've
nothing to do with the police."

"I was on the lawn," Caroline told him

shortly. She shivered. "I feel rather cold, I think I'll go back."

Perhaps she hoped he would leave her, but Craig turned too, and they headed back towards the house.

"There was a girl called Mary Whittaker here when Randall was killed," he remarked. "Do you know what happened to her?"

"I believe she committed suicide years ago. I hardly knew her."

They reached the house and Caroline went into the drawing-room. Craig decided he would prefer solitude to think to the more or less open hostility of the Laxtons and the Fenns, and made for the library. Granger had departed some time before.

One thing he knew, Caroline hadn't been telling the truth, at least not the whole truth, when she said she was on the lawn this afternoon. She might have been there earlier, but when he looked that way after he and Gail finished playing tennis there was no sign of her. And that must have been within a few minutes of Jordan's being shot.

Craig wasn't left to enjoy his solitude for long, he had been in the library only a few minutes when the door opened and Charles Laxton walked in.

"I wanted a word with you in private," the MP explained.

"Oh?" Craig said. "I got the feeling I wasn't exactly welcome company where you were concerned."

"Eh? What?" Laxton looked startled.

"Skip it."

There was a moment's silence while Laxton considered whether to put this insolent young upstart in his place. In the end he decided not to try, antagonising Craig would achieve nothing just now.

"My wife tells me she's hired you to find out what Jordan was planning," he said.

"More or less."

"Well, I've come to tell you she's changed her mind. The police are handling this shocking business and we both feel we can rely on them to do their job. It's no reflection on you personally, but if you start asking the same people questions, you're bound to end up getting in their way, and we couldn't be responsible for that. You used to be in the police, you'll agree, eh?"

It occurred to Craig that some men he knew,

and women too, would have told him bluntly the job was cancelled and forget it, but even now Laxton couldn't forget he was a politician and he had to hedge his instructions round with specious explanations. Because Craig had no doubt they were specious, it was as plain as a pikestaff Laxton didn't want him asking questions because of what he might discover. He would probably try to ham-string Granger if he thought he could.

"I'd have thought you'd have backed private enterprise," he observed lightly. Laxton stared at him. "All right, Mrs. Laxton hired me, as you put it. If she wants me to stop, she'll have to tell me so herself."

The MP looked as if he was going to lose his temper, but he restrained himself. "I take it you're not deliberately being offensive," he said.

Craig grinned without humour. "People tell me I succeed without trying," he replied cheerfully. "Usually they're people who have a good reason for being offended. Does Mrs. Laxton know you want me to stop?"

There was a noticeable pause before Laxton answered, "No."

"Yet she's still changed her mind? If you

125

don't tell her, I shall; she's a right to know. And when she does, won't she wonder what it is you're so anxious nobody shall find out about?"

"You—" Laxton began.

"Get lost," Craig told him. He was enjoying himself; it wasn't often the chance came to cut people like Laxton down to size. "I'm working for your wife; until she tells me to stop I go on working for her. And don't forget, it's my taxes help pay you, I'm not your lackey. You can help or do the other thing, just as you like." Craig paused. "And I shall go on asking questions whether she pays me to or not, because Micky Jordan invited me here too, and I want to know who killed him and why."

This time the silence lasted longer. Then Laxton said quietly, "I suppose that's fair."

"You're prepared to talk?" He nodded. "Right, I want to know everything you can remember about the weekend Randall was murdered."

Laxton hadn't quite relaxed yet, but his manner was calmer and Craig reckoned he would learn more by encouraging him to talk than by pressing him. Antagonised, the MP would probably take refuge in a stubborn silence. As it was his hostility seemed to have exhausted itself.

"It's odd," he remarked, "I thought I'd almost forgotten that weekend, but now it's all come back."

"Memory's a funny thing," Craig agreed. In a more businesslike tone he went on, "Apart from the Randalls there were eight people here, right?"

Laxton thought. "Lorraine, Caroline, Bateman, Jane Marsh, Mary Whittaker, Fenn, me. That's seven."

"What about Phillipson?"

"I'd forgotten him. He was the sort of fellow people always do forget."

"What was the atmosphere like?"

"Atmosphere? All right, I suppose."

"No tension you could tell?"

"Not that I remember. It was all pretty easy-going—you know, light hearted—until what happened."

"Did the Randalls seem on good terms?"

"As far as you could see, they did." Perhaps he felt on safer ground talking about what had happened thirty years ago, whatever the reason Laxton was talking more freely now.

"Did you have any doubt that Susan Randall was guilty?"

Laxton looked unhappy. "It was a shock. It didn't seem possible she could have done a thing like that, but—well, the police were sure. I don't mind telling you, it was a relief when she was reprieved."

And this was the man who wanted the death penalty restored, Craig thought. On the one occasion when the consequences had touched him personally his resolution had faltered. "Where were you all when Randall was shot?" he asked.

"I'd been playing tennis with Lorraine against Mary Whittaker and Phillipson," Laxton replied. "Caroline had wandered off, she didn't like tennis. It was damned hot and when we finished the second set Fenn and Jane Marsh played the other two and I came in to get some drinks."

Craig wondered why the MP had hesitated over the last few words. "Where was Bateman?" he enquired.

"He'd sloped off somewhere while we were playing that set; he'd played the first with Lorraine or Jane. I can't remember now, it was a long time ago."

"You came alone for the drinks?"

"Yes." Laxton's tone had suddenly become blustering. "What's all this got to do with who killed Jordan?"

"It may have a lot," Craig told him. "Where was Lorraine?"

"She followed me in here. I—" Laxton stopped abruptly.

"Where were the drinks? In the dining room? Or did you find the Randalls' housekeeper or a maid?"

"Why?"

"If it was so hot the windows must have been open. Randall was shot with a ·38 revolver; that would make a lot of noise. Did you hear the shot?"

"Not to notice it."

"I see," Craig said coolly.

"What do you mean, you see?" the MP demanded aggressively. It seemed that embarrassment was making him angry.

"Do you want me to spell it out?"

Their eyes met. Little crimson patches stained Laxton's thin cheeks.

"You can think what you like," he said.

"How did you hear what had happened?" Craig asked him.

"One of the others came in and told us. Phillipson, I think." Again Laxton seemed unsure of himself. "It was a terrible shock for Caroline."

"Finding his body?"

"Yes. Yes, of course." Laxton appeared to regret having said anything, and Craig was pretty sure that wasn't what he had really meant.

Caroline and Randall were having an affair. No wonder she had screamed when she found Lorraine standing looking down at Micky Jordan's body this afternoon, history repeating itself in such a grisly fashion would have been more than enough for most people. Or had there been more to it than that? Guilt, like memory, played strange tricks.

"What sort of man was Bateman?" Craig asked.

Laxton hesitated. "Poor sort of fellow, I thought. Weak. You might not think it to look at her now, but Caroline was the one who wore the trousers there. After their marriage broke up he went to pieces. Started drinking. In the end he piled his car up and was killed."

"And Caroline married again?"

"Oh, she was already married by then. She

divorced Bateman soon after the business here." With unexpected irony Laxton added, "Men were still expected to behave like gentlemen and let their wives divorce them in those days. Even if the wives had been sleeping around all over the place. Lot of nonsense. But Rupert was a Roman, I daresay that had something to do with it; he wouldn't divorce Caroline but it was all right if she divorced him and he didn't marry again. Anyway, she came out of it very nicely, he paid her most of everything he had."

"How well did you know Lorraine?" Craig asked. He was convinced the MP and the actress had been more than merely friends, hence Laxton's embarrassment a few minutes ago. And if Lorraine had followed him into the house almost immediately, she couldn't have shot Randall. Craig wondered how long it had been before Phillipson found them.

Laxton had seemed oddly embarrassed by Lorraine's presence ever since their meeting yesterday evening, yet he was hardly able to take his eyes off her when his wife wasn't watching. For her part, Lorraine's manner to him had been gently amused and almost tender.

"I was fond of her," Laxton replied stiffly. "I think she quite liked me."

"And Randall wanted her."

"He didn't make any secret of it. It was a sort of joke to him," the MP said bitterly. "Then she went off to Hollywood, I met Elizabeth, and that was that. We've been very happy," he added defensively.

Craig suspected he had been more in love with Lorraine than she was with him. Now they had met again after all these years and he was reliving his youth. He had had a pretty strong motive for killing Randall, but the police must have satisfied themselves he was innocent.

"How long had you known Jordan?" Craig asked.

"Four or five months. But we'd only met a few times; he wasn't a type I care for."

"You accepted his invitation this weekend."

"There was a suggestion he wanted to put something to me," Laxton said, looking uncomfortable.

"Something?"

"A directorship of one of his companies. Something like that. It was only a hint, we hadn't talked about it."

Craig looked the MP in the eyes. "What is it you're so afraid I'll find out?" he asked.

"Afraid? What do you mean? I'm not afraid

of anything." Laxton's tone lacked conviction. "Why should I be?"

"I've no idea. But you don't want me asking questions, do you?"

Anger—real or assumed, Craig wasn't sure which—darkened the older man's complexion again. "I'm not staying here to listen to your innuendoes," he said. Standing up, he started towards the door.

"Where were you when Jordan was killed?" Craig asked.

Laxton turned. "My wife and I were looking at the roses. She's rather an expert. We have a lot at our cottage in the country and she was interested in some of the varieties here."

"Did you see anybody go past?"

There was a second's hesitation before the MP said, "Lorraine went along the path to the wood."

"We know that. Did you see Caroline or any of the others?"

"No." Laxton paused, and when he spoke again it was almost plaintively. "It's thirty years since Randall was shot, why does it all have to be raked up again?" Turning, he went out of the room.

Perhaps unknowingly, Craig reflected,

Laxton had put his finger on one of the most puzzling features of the whole business: what could be so dangerous after all this time that someone had been driven to murder because of it?

"How serious was it?" Fenn asked hopelessly.

"Serious?" Gabriella repeated. "It was serious with 'im."

"Can't you be honest even about that?"

Gabriella eyed her husband thoughtfully and shrugged. "'Ow can you measure love?" she demanded theatrically. Then her expression softened. "Does it matter so much what I do, Simon?"

"You know it does," Fenn answered miserably.

"It was only a game. A woman likes to know men think she is attractive."

Jordan had said something like that, Fenn told himself. He had remarked that what he was planning for this afternoon was only a sort of game.

"Anyway, it was over," Gabriella went on. "Until this weekend I 'adn't seen Miles for more than two months, why need 'e make any difference to us? We are just like we 'ave always been."

"Can't you see why?" Fenn stood up from the edge of the bed and walked over to his wife. "Sometimes I wish I didn't, but I can't help the way I feel about you," he muttered.

For a moment it seemed they understood each other, then Fenn turned away. "Where did you go this afternoon?" he demanded.

"I didn't go anywhere," Gabriella retorted.

"I saw you. You put on that robe thing and went along the path towards the wood. Did you go to see Jordan?"

"No. No, I didn't." Gabriella looked alarmed. "I went for a little walk, that's all. As far as the beginning of the wood. I didn't go near the summerhouse. Where did you go, Simon?"

"To get something from the car."

"You think the police will believe that?"

"I don't care whether they believe it or not." Fenn knew it was a lie and he cared very much. Unintentionally, probably without realizing what she was doing, Gabriella had succeeded in making it seem he had had a stronger motive for killing Jordan than anyone.

"I wish I knew who Craig really is," he

muttered, half to himself. He wasn't sure why not knowing bothered him so much, but Jordan must have invited Craig here for a reason, and he hadn't trusted Jordan an inch. Another thought occurred to him. "That girl Gail's frightened," he observed.

"Gail!" Gabriella snorted, her eyes glittering.

Fenn saw it and felt uneasy. "What do you know?" he demanded.

"What makes you think I know anything?" Gabriella countered defensively.

"Because you look so pleased with yourself," Fenn told her. He wished devoutly he hadn't let her persuade him into coming this weekend. She was like a child, half the time she didn't see the consequences of her actions.

Gabriella laughed quietly.

There were signs of strain on Lorraine Maxwell's carefully made-up features, but she sat upright in her chair and regarded Craig steadily. He reflected that he must have seen a score of pictures of her posed like that, the same half-smile touching the corners of her perfect mouth. A little slimmer then, it was true, but otherwise hardly changed. Perhaps the pose, leaning very slightly to her right, right forearm raised, the hand drooping gracefully an inch or two below her chin, was second nature to her now. Possibly it always had been.

"Miles was killed because of what he intended doing," she said calmly. "He was a fool to go ahead with it."

"With what?" Craig asked.

"Whatever it was."

"Do you know?"

The actress shook her head and the diamonds in her ears caught the light. She had changed into a simple dress of some dark green material patterned with black that showed off the enamelled perfection of her skin yet was decently subdued for the circumstances. "No, he wouldn't tell me."

"You asked him this morning, didn't you?" Craig said.

"Yes."

"What do you think he was planning?"

"A reconstruction of what happened before, I guess. But I really don't know. Maybe he had some crazy notion of filming it for his programme. That or . . ." The sentence died away.

"Or what?" Craig enquired.

"A trial," Lorraine said. "That would have been worse. Much worse. Poor Miles."

"Why was he so set on it?" Craig asked. "What did he know?"

Lorraine eyed him as if she was trying to make up her mind how much to tell him. "I don't know he *knew* anything," she said. "Maybe that didn't matter to him."

Craig felt that he was floundering out of his depth. "What do you mean?" he asked.

"It was what he felt that counted," Lorraine said. "The injustice—and the horror. All he was talking about before dinner yesterday evening, he'd experienced that personally. Miles was Susan Randall's son."

9

HER son! It was impossible, Craig told himself. True, the old newspaper reports he had read after Jordan's visit to his office had mentioned a five-year-old boy, but it had never occurred to him Miles Jordan could be that child. He had known him when he was Micky, a schoolboy living with his parents in a quiet road in Bayswater. His father was a writer and broadcaster and his mother had some job in publishing. They could probably have afforded to send him to a public school like most of their friends' children, but they had Leftish views and instead he had gone to Lancaster Grove Comprehensive. It didn't seem to have harmed his prospects.

Craig had met his parents once when Micky took him home to tea. Nice people they had seemed to him at the age of—what was it? Thirteen?—but even then he had sensed they weren't at their ease with him. They hadn't known how to talk to the son of a corner shopkeeper and their awkwardness had been transmitted to him.

Yet Lorraine seemed sure.

"I was at school with him," he protested. "I met his parents."

"Sure. But that was later, right?" Craig nodded. "After Nigel was killed Susan's sister and her husband took Michael to live with them. I believe they adopted him as soon as they could. He stopped being Michael Randall and became Michael Jordan."

"Did he know who he was?"

"Not then; he found out a few months ago. After his uncle died. I'd say that's when he bought this house."

He had his reasons, Craig thought. "You knew at dinner yesterday, didn't you?" he said. "I saw your face when I called him Micky; the others were surprised but you weren't."

"I'd guessed. There was something about him round the eyes—and he had his mother's colouring. I noticed them in New York and I couldn't think who they reminded me of. Then, when I came over to England and got his invitation it clicked. Having him live in Lower Marking too seemed like too much of a coincidence. I kind of challenged him this morning and he told me."

"But not what he meant to do?"

"No."

"The others didn't notice anything," Craig observed.

"Maybe not. Or perhaps they just kept it to themselves. I knew Susan better than Caroline or Charles."

She was more observant too, Craig suspected. "How did you come to meet him in New York?" he asked.

"About three months ago I was doing a play on Broadway. It didn't run too long." Lorraine grimaced. "Miles was over there at the same time and I knew the people he was staying with, Katie and Howard Barnfield. Katie called me up one day and said they were throwing a party for him and would I go. He was one of the biggest names in TV in Britain and he wanted to meet me.

"I thought Katie was making it up, but I liked her, so I went." Lorraine gave an amused little laugh. "He kind of made a play for me. He did it very sweetly and I knew there wasn't anything in it, but hell, I'm not past liking that sort of thing. It ended with him asking me out to lunch the day before he flew home and I went. I told him I was coming over to England soon and he made me promise I'd look him up. When I saw his address on the invitation it really shook me. I came down one day to take a look. When I found it was the Randalls' old place I got a kind of eerie feeling, I don't mind telling you, Alan. I was almost sure then.

"He told me this morning he just remembered his mother. I guess he was very fond of her, more than he was of his father—he didn't see so much of Nigel—and over the years she became just a memory he fantasised about a bit. His uncle and aunt had told him she'd died soon after his father. Maybe Susan asked them to; that would have been like her. He was too young to understand anything about the murder and there was nothing to tell him. It wasn't the sort of case people remember.

"I went to see Susan once, in prison after—" Lorraine paused, then went on, "after she was reprieved. She told me then she thought the best thing would be for the Jordans to adopt Michael. I think, once she knew they weren't going to—to hang her the worst thing was knowing that she might never see him again.

"I went to the States in March, '56. I wrote

once or twice, but she didn't answer and I thought maybe she didn't want to be reminded, so I stopped. After I came back to England I found she'd died a few years later. Michael's uncle died last year. His aunt had been dead three years then and when everything was being sorted out he found the papers to do with his adoption and other things. The money Nigel and Susan left had been put in a trust fund so he never knew where the income came from. After he found the papers he started asking questions and discovered about the murder and the trial. It must have been kind of traumatic for him."

Craig reckoned that was probably an understatement. Micky was proud.

"Why did you go to the summerhouse this afternoon?" he asked.

"To try to persuade him to give up whatever crazy idea he'd got."

"And he was dead when you got there?"

Lorraine nodded. "I couldn't believe it. It was just like that other time all over again. And then Caroline coming along . . ."

"Not quite like the other time," Craig said.

"How was it different?"

"There was no gun this time." Craig paused. "Was there?"

"No, there wasn't." Lorraine looked surprised. "You know, I never thought of that."

Craig wondered whether she was telling the truth—and if not why not.

"How well did you know the people who were here then?" he asked.

"Susan and Nigel quite well, not the others. I'd met them a few times, we had the same friends and went to the same parties. That sort of thing."

"There was a girl called Mary Whittaker," Craig said.

"Was there?" The actress looked as if she genuinely couldn't remember. "Maybe she was one of Nigel's girl friends. He was making rather a nuisance of himself."

"With you? Did his wife mind?"

"Not in the way you mean; she knew I wasn't interested. Anyway he wasn't what you'd call the constant type and he found somebody who was more responsive."

"Caroline."

"You see too much," Lorraine said. "I shall have to be careful."

"And she found Susan Randall in the summerhouse looking down at his dead body. Just like she found you looking at Micky this afternoon. No wonder she screamed."

"Poor Caroline."

"Yes, poor Caroline," Craig agreed. "Do you like her?"

"No."

"Why not?"

"I don't see that's really any of your concern but I'll tell you. We don't have much in common. And I don't like women who are really tough but pretend to be helpless. They're dishonest."

Craig grinned. "Do you remember where you all were when Randall was shot?" he asked.

Lorraine regarded him quizzically. "You ask an awful lot of questions, Alan."

"I know."

"And all about something that happened nearly thirty years ago."

"I'm like you, I think that's what it's all about."

"And the Superintendent? What does he think?"

"He's still sure Susan Randall was guilty."

There was a second's pause before Lorraine

145

said, "Caroline and Rupert said they were in the wood. Caroline told everybody she'd been for a walk by the river but I always thought she was with Nigel." She stopped. "Maybe you'd best forget that, I could be wrong. Peter and Roger Phillipson were playing tennis with the other two girls. Just like you were this afternoon with Gail. That made it seem worse—as if somebody was playing some kind of sadistic practical joke."

"That leaves two people," Craig said evenly.

"That's right. You know, don't you? I was with Charles, here in the house. He was one reason I wasn't interested in Nigel. I guess you find that hard to believe now, but he was different then, young and charming." Lorraine sighed gently. "Michael was convinced his mother didn't kill his father. That's what all this was about."

"He was going to show who did?"

"Something like that, maybe."

"Did he drop any hint who it was?"

"No."

"And what about you?" Craig asked. "Who do you think did it?"

"I don't know. But I think he was right." Lorraine paused. "Or maybe I only hope; I

146

liked Susan too much to want her to have done a thing like that. I know what they say about everybody being capable of murder, and God knows she had plenty of cause to shoot him, I just can't believe she would have deliberately hurt anybody, let alone kill them. For one thing, she wasn't the jealous type, and she was level headed. If she'd decided she'd had enough and couldn't take any more, she'd have told Nigel and left him."

"And if Randall had told her he wouldn't support her?" Craig asked. "It wasn't so easy for wives to walk out then, was it?"

"That wouldn't have worried her, she wasn't exactly on the bread line."

For a moment there was silence in the room. Outside the sun had almost set, but neither of the people there seemed to notice that the light had faded and now it was half dark.

"Granger worked on the case and he says there wasn't any doubt she was guilty," Craig said.

Lorraine sketched a shrug. "It isn't easy to admit you were wrong and start again from the beginning," she commented. "Some people really can convince themselves the easy way is the right one. It must happen with the police here, just like anywhere else. They're human. Besides the Superintendent must be about ready to retire, he won't want anything fouling things up for him now."

Craig was beginning to think she could, just possibly, be right. Because the odds were still stacked against Susan Randall's having been innocent.

"Why did Mrs. Randall suddenly decide to go out and leave everybody like that?" he asked.

Lorraine hesitated. "She had a boy friend," she said at last. "He lived a few miles away and Susan was very much in love with him. His mother phoned her that afternoon to say he'd been knocked down by a car and rushed to hospital."

"What happened to him?" Craig asked. "Nobody's mentioned him before."

"He died just before the trial. I don't know whether Susan told her lawyers about him. Maybe they decided it would count against her if it came out. I've wondered since if his dying had anything to do with her not fighting harder."

"Did you know him?"

"I met him twice. He was a solicitor, a rather

148

sweet, kind sort of man. All the things Nigel wasn't."

For a moment neither of them spoke, then Craig said, "If the murders are connected, it means somebody knew what Jordan was planning to do and was frightened enough to kill to stop him. Somebody who had something to hide going back thirty years. You say you and Charles Laxton were together when Randall was shot: you know what that means, don't you?"

"Yes," Lorraine agreed, her tone devoid of expression.

When she had gone Craig sat staring into the shadows. Working for himself was a new experience. In the past he had been allotted tasks as part of the overall pattern of an investigation and discussed its progress with other people, here he was on his own with no help from the resources of a modern police force and no more knowledge of what Granger's men were turning up than the Superintendent cared to pass on to him. And that was unlikely to be much.

He didn't blame the local man. Why should Granger tell an outsider—and one who, as a guest in the house, must be a potential suspect

—anything? Also he had made his dislike very clear: Craig was an ex-copper and therefore in the nature of things not to be trusted.

So he must use his head.

Start from the beginning, he told himself. There must be a link between the murders, find it and hopefully everything would begin to fall into place. The key to Jordan's death was something that had happened in 1954. Had he unearthed some new evidence which suggested, maybe even proved, his mother didn't kill his father? Evidence which also, perhaps, proved who did?

Lorraine had seen that if she and Laxton were together in the house when Randall was shot, the only other logical suspect was Caroline Rogers. True Fenn's parents had been here that other fateful weekend, but it would be stretching probability too much to suggest that could give him a motive. Anyway, they had been playing tennis, neither of them could have shot Randall.

Caroline had gone out of her way to tell him her relationship with Randall had ended before that weekend, but Lorraine had implied that, on the contrary, it was new. Craig was prepared to believe Caroline was capable of murder if the motive were compelling enough and she was confident of getting away with it, but he couldn't see what motive she could have had for killing Randall.

Had Lorraine and Laxton both lied? If so, neither of them had an alibi for Randall's murder.

Start again, Craig thought. But where was the beginning to start from?

While he was talking to Granger an idea had occurred to him. It was too vague to be put into words, little more than a feeling that the whole set-up was too theatrical. It was almost as if someone had contrived it deliberately to suggest a link between the two murders when none existed.

If there were no link, then the field was a good deal wider. Take Fenn, he was jealous and neurotic. He had made no secret of his dislike for his host, and his wife's behaviour, flaunting her affair with Jordan, might have provoked a more stable man than he was to violence. As for Gabriella, whatever she pretended to believe, she must know that Jordan had used her to scrape an acquaintance with her husband, and that when he achieved it he had lost interest in her. This weekend he had thrown Gail in her face almost as blatantly as she had thrown him in Fenn's. For a woman with her temperament that could have been motive enough.

Elizabeth Laxton, too, might have contemplated murder if she believed Jordan was a threat to her husband. But Gail was here only because she was Jordan's current girl friend. True, she could have been lying, and it wasn't her but Micky who wanted to terminate their relationship, but it seemed unlikely.

Even Sandra couldn't be forgotten, for unless he had made a will since they separated she would presumably inherit a large part of whatever he had left.

Craig's thoughts took a different turn. Where had Willy Davies kept his gun? The obvious places were the old stables with their two unconverted rooms adjoining the garage and the flat. Wherever it was, not many of this weekend's guests could be expected to know even that he had a gun, let alone where he kept it. The Fenns had stayed here before, they might know, and Gail too perhaps. Sandra almost certainly knew. But not the others.

When he and Gail changed ends after their first set Gabriella was still stretched out on one of the loungers beside the pool, but Fenn was walking towards the stable block. If he had taken Davies's rifle and carried it down to the river, he must have gone by the other path, the one Sandra was to take a few minutes later. That way he would have run less risk of meeting anybody, and it would explain why the Laxtons hadn't seen him pass. All the same, he would have been taking a considerable chance, for a man in a sports shirt couldn't conceal even a light ·22 rifle easily.

The next time Craig looked Gabriella had disappeared. Nobody, he thought, possessed any sort of alibi. People had been wandering about all over the place, and while the Laxtons claimed they were together on the lawn, there had been sufficient time for one of them to slip down to the summerhouse, shoot Jordan, and return without being noticed. Craig didn't doubt that both of them were quite capable of lying to protect the other.

The only person who had been seen actually heading for the wood was Lorraine. Sandra had been talking to Mrs. Davies, but where had Willy been? He was a nutter, goodness only knew what twisted motive he might have dreamed up for shooting his employer. And, after all, it was almost certainly his gun the murderer had used.

Craig didn't envy Granger.

Standing up, he stretched and went out to the verandah. It was lighter here, the twilight only just beginning to fade into dusk, and the discordantly cheerful sounds of a fair floated up from the village. Down there people were going about their normal lives, he reflected, unaware that only half a mile away a man whose face was as familiar to many of them as their neighbour's had been murdered. No doubt they would get a vicarious thrill when they read about it in the papers.

That was something else they would have to face, the presence and questions of the Press. Any time now the reporters would start arriving.

"What's happening?"

Craig turned. Sandra had come out of the house and was standing a few feet away, her arms and face pale in the half light and her dark hair blending into the shadows.

"I don't know," he replied.

"It's rather unnerving, isn't it? Not knowing what they're doing, I mean. But I suppose you're used to it."

"Unnerving?" Craig asked.

Sandra came nearer. He could see her eyes now and smell her perfume.

"Does that sound like an admission of guilt? Disconcerting then. They're doing things, discovering things which may alter all our lives, and we don't know."

"I hadn't thought of it like that," Craig admitted. "To the police it's just a job to be done. You can't let yourself get emotionally involved with the people in a case any more than a surgeon can with his patients. He'd never make the first incision if he did. Where are the others?"

"Caroline and Simon are playing bridge with the Laxtons. I think Simon's rapidly driving Caroline mad, he's not very good and she takes it terribly seriously." Sandra paused, looking across the wide sweep of the lawn. "I'm going to stay here tonight and move back properly as soon as I can."

"Oh?" Craig wondered why she had told him.

"It's the sensible thing to do. There are bound to be all sorts of things to deal with and it'll be easier if I'm on the spot."

"It seems a good idea."

There was a brief silence. Craig thought that he felt at his ease with Sandra. She was calm and matter-of-fact, the opposite of Caroline and Gabriella, yet he suspected she was capable of deep feelings. She was attractive, too.

"Where was everybody when—when it happened?" she asked him. "I feel I'm involved, but I don't know anything because I wasn't here and nobody wants to talk about it."

"They weren't doing anything much," Craig told her. "Micky said he had to do some work. Gail and I played a couple of sets of tennis, the Fenns were sun-bathing by the pool and the others were sitting on the verandah. After a while they started moving about; the Laxtons went to look at the roses and the Fenns drifted off somewhere."

"And then?" Sandra asked, her voice almost a whisper.

"I heard Caroline scream."

"Oh God!" For a second or two Sandra said nothing, then she asked, "Do you mind if we walk? I can't stand just hanging about waiting any longer. I must do something, even if it's only walking round the garden."

"That's all right," Craig agreed. He was

surprised at the pleasure he felt because she had suggested it.

They walked past the end of the house and the outbuildings to the wall which bounded the grounds on the east. Just inside the wall there was a path leading past the vegetable garden towards the swimming pool and they took it, walking slowly and for much of the time in silence. Craig was very conscious of Sandra close to him, and had to resist the temptation to put his arm round her.

Surely she must know this had been Micky's home when he was a little boy, he thought. Not that it made any difference.

"Did Micky ever talk about when he was a kid?" he enquired.

"Not really. He always said he couldn't remember much about it." Sandra stopped and turned towards him, her face almost lost in the shadows; darkness was falling rapidly now. "You think he was shot because of something to do with what happened here before, to that man Randall, don't you?" she asked.

So she still didn't know, Craig thought. Micky hadn't told her when he learnt the truth about himself after his uncle's death, and

Lorraine had said nothing. But she knew his real name was Michael.

"Yes," he answered, "I do. That's why the police will want to find out what he was planning for this weekend." They walked on. "How long have the Davieses worked for you?"

"Since soon after we were married. You know Willy used to work at the studios?"

"Yes, Micky told me. There was an accident, a man was injured and people blamed him."

"He told you about that, did he? Miles always swore it really was an accident, and I expect it was. But Willy has a terrible temper and he's unpredictable. I don't mean he's unbalanced, but . . ." Sandra hesitated. "He frightens me sometimes."

"He frightened me this morning," Craig told her. "He nearly shot me."

"*You*? Where?"

"In the wood."

"I expect he was after pigeons. He's got a thing about them eating his plants."

"He said he was. Do I look like a pigeon?"

Sandra smiled. "Not very."

"You know his gun's disappeared, don't you?"

"Yes."

"Where does he keep it?"

"Somewhere in the old stables, I believe. I don't know where exactly. I suppose the police think whoever killed Miles used it?"

"I suppose so," Craig agreed. "How did he and Willy get on?" Sandra hesitated again before she answered, taking special care over choosing her words. "All right as a rule. Willy was grateful to Miles, but he gets uptight sometimes."

"You mean they had rows?"

"Not often. And I don't think they were very serious." They had circled the house and back on the verandah Sandra said simply, "Thank you, Alan, I feel better now."

"I'm glad."

Perhaps there was something in Craig's tone of which he was unaware, for in the light from the hall he could see her expression of surprise.

"It was all over between Miles and me, you know," she said quietly. "We were still good friends, but we'd never have got together again." In a different tone she added, "I must get back, they'll be wondering where I am."

She entered the house and Craig, feeling strangely unsettled, followed. But when she went into the drawing-room he walked farther along the hall to the library, opened the door and walked in.

Elizabeth Laxton was standing behind Jordan's desk. She was bending over and Craig was almost sure he had heard the tiny shuffling sound of a well fitting drawer being closed. As he came towards her she looked up and their eyes met.

"I was looking for some writing paper," she said coolly.

He let it pass. There seemed no point in his saying anything, it was so palpably a lie.

Elizabeth walked to the door. As she passed him he noticed a faint flush on her usually sallow cheeks and he suspected it was caused more by anger that he of all people had caught her out than shame at what she had been doing. He wondered if she knew quite what she was looking for. Very likely not, and she had just hoped that if Jordan possessed anything in writing which might harm her husband, it would be here and she could destroy it.

He could imagine her insisting she be the one to look, because if she were found it would matter less than Laxton's being caught rifling Jordan's desk. Women like Elizabeth possessed that sort of courage.

Waiting until the door had closed behind her, he crossed to the desk himself and opened the drawers quickly one after the other. He found nothing. Elizabeth had had no time to destroy anything and she had been empty handed when she left the room, so it looked as if there had been nothing here for her to find.

Unless one of Granger's men had discovered it first.

10

IT was very quiet. Craig glanced at his watch on the bedside table; it said ten minutes past seven. Slipping out of bed, he crossed to the window and looked out. Yesterday's storm hadn't broken the spell of fine weather and already the sun was breaking through a haze with the promise of another hot day. Craig, who had slept well, wondered how many other people in the house could say the same.

When he had washed and shaved he slipped on a shirt and a pair of trousers, put his wallet and keys in his pocket and went quickly down the stairs. Apparently the Davieses too slept later on Sundays, there was no sound as he crossed the hall, let himself out of the house and walked silently along the verandah towards the garage. On his right the lawn was silver-grey with dew. A squirrel was poised, alert, halfway to the pergola. Hearing him as he stepped on to the gravel, it sped off in the direction of the hedge.

Craig had reached the corner of the stable

block before he saw the uniformed constable standing in the shadows. As he approached, the policeman stepped forward.

"Good morning, sir," he said.

"'Morning," Craig returned. "It looks like being another fine day."

"May I ask where you're going, sir?" The constable looked about twenty, Craig thought.

"Out," he said.

"The Superintendent would be obliged if everybody stayed near the house today, sir."

"Oh? Well, if he asks, tell him I've gone to see the vicar and I'll be back later," Craig said.

"I'm afraid I can't let you go, sir."

The silence was like a void between them. Craig was two inches taller than the younger man who had to look up slightly to meet his eye.

"Are you detaining me?" he asked.

"Detaining you?" The constable looked puzzled.

"Either you are or I'm free to go where I like."

The peak of his helmet obscured a good deal of the policeman's face, but it didn't conceal his uncertainty. Craig felt rather sorry for him. He started to heave on the garage door and saw the lad reach out a hand to prevent him, then draw it back.

The bottom of the wooden door grated on the gravel. Over it two windows in the Davieses' flat were open. If the gardener kept his gun here it would have been a simple matter for somebody to slip in and take it while he and his wife were working, he in the gardens and she in the house, Craig reflected. But yesterday was Saturday, had Davies been working?

He backed the Dolomite out, turned it and started down the drive. There was another policeman on duty where it met the road, but he did no more than glance at the car as Craig slowed and turned left towards the village. So far, it seemed, the Press hadn't got hold of the story, but any time now the reporters and photographers would start to gather.

Once through Lower Marking Craig headed for the motorway. At this time on a fine Sunday morning in July most people who were about were making for the coast or the country and there was very little traffic going towards London. It took him only a little over an hour to reach the City. Parking outside his office, he locked the car and climbed the three flights of stairs. The building had the hollow feel offices acquire when they are unoccupied and his foot-steps on the stone treads sounded unnaturally loud.

There was a message on his answering machine: Vigors, an inquiry agent in Brighton, had rung to report that Hollins had worked the town for two or three weeks, then moved on. For some reason his last landlady was convinced he had gone to Bournemouth, but in Vigors' opinion it could just as well be Torquay or Llandudno. Working the resorts during the season, Craig thought disgustedly. No doubt by now he had removed more cheque books and credit cards from their careless owners.

For the next twenty minutes Craig busied himself with reference books, making occasional notes on a pad. Then he studied a road atlas, checking routes and calculating mileages. Finally he put the notes in his pocket, locked up and returned to his car.

"Where's he gone?" Granger demanded. He was angry, and he didn't care who knew it. He had given instructions that he wanted the people in the house to remain within reach and this smart alec ex-copper had conned young Frost into letting him go without even finding out where. The vicar! Granger practically snorted with disgust.

"He'll be back," Franklin said consolingly. "He's left all his stuff behind."

"What the hell's that got to do with it?"

Franklin knew better than to argue. He was a dark, lean man of 36—"one of your technical blokes" in Granger's slightly scornful phraseology—and he had learnt long ago that sometimes when one's superiors asked questions they neither expected nor wanted to be answered.

The two men were sitting in the mobile incident room.

"I don't like ex-coppers," Granger growled. "You can't trust 'em." Catching the Inspector's eye and noticing a slightly sardonic light in it, he added impatiently, "Not the ones who've retired properly, I mean the ones who've been kicked out or resigned. Coppers don't resign if there's nothing wrong with them."

"I had a word with a chap I know in the Met," Franklin volunteered.

"Oh? What's he say?"

"According to him, Craig was forced out because he started shooting his mouth off about a bent sergeant the super was covering up for.

He wouldn't shut up, so they made sure nobody would take any notice of him."

Granger remembered what Craig had said about superintendents. "You think it's true?" he asked.

"The chap I spoke to reckoned it was. He said Craig was a good d/s. They'd worked together."

Granger groaned. He hated corruption of any sort and crooked policemen most of all.

"You think he's right and this business is tied up with the Randall case, guv?" Franklin asked.

"The time to start getting theories is when you've collected all the information you can," Granger told him sourly. "Make up your mind too soon and you can't see the wood for the trees. You should know that by now."

"Yes, guv," Franklin said contritely.

"How much longer will it take those frogs to finish the river?" Granger demanded.

Two frogmen were searching the bed of the stream for some distance on each side of the summerhouse in the hope, fading fast as far as the Superintendent was concerned, of finding Willy Davies' rifle and anything else that might conceivably throw any light on Jordan's death.

With Sandra's consent other men had searched the house and were now engaged in combing the gardens and the wood. So far they had found nothing.

"Another hour or two, I should think," Franklin said. He wondered what sort of reception he would get from his wife when he finally reached home. Whenever that was; this looked like being another long and tedious day. Mary had been in a right two and eight this morning because she and the kids had been looking forward to a day at Brighton and he couldn't take them. He'd suggested they go without him, but that hadn't gone down very well either.

Granger groaned again and looked across at a woman constable who was busy with a card index. "What about some more tea, love?" he called.

"I've got to talk to you," Laxton said.

Charles looked worried, Lorraine thought. Poor Charles, he did take himself and his position seriously; it was hard to believe he was the same man she had known thirty years ago. Was that Elizabeth's doing, or would he have turned out like this even if he hadn't married her?

"Sure, honey," she agreed. Why was it that when she was speaking to him her American accent broadened almost unconsciously? "Here?"

Laxton glanced round the verandah. The windows were open.

"No, somewhere more private," he said. "There won't be anyone in the wood."

"Except the police." Lorraine stood up. This morning she was wearing a pale yellow dress and white, high-heeled sandals. Her make-up was more restrained and, apart from her rings, her only jewellery was a pair of tiny earstuds. "Okay, we can try. If they're still there we can walk along the bank, I guess. It'll be quite like old times, Charles."

There was a hint of mischief in the words, but Laxton said nothing. Looking back brought him more regrets than joy these days. He had started in politics with so much hope and ambition, but somehow the brightness had faded, time had slipped past, and he had never been offered a job in government. The last few years there had been times when he felt life was passing him by. In the old days 61 had been no great age for an MP with hopes of office, nowadays even the PM seemed to share the common obsession with youth, and years of loyal support counted for nothing. It was hard for him to accept that he would never achieve anything now, that the years which had gone were lost for ever and opportunity was never coming.

"Where's Elizabeth?" Lorraine asked.

"Getting ready for church. She goes every Sunday, she wouldn't let a little thing like a murder put her off."

"That sounded kind of cynical. Rather unkind too."

"Yes, I suppose it did. Sorry. We're very happy, you know."

"Good."

If there was a note of irony in Lorraine's voice, Laxton didn't notice it. They walked on, through the arch to the wood.

It was blessedly cool here in the trees.

"Why is the scent of pines so evocative?" Lorraine asked musingly.

"Eh?"

She laughed gently. "Nothing Charles. I was just being fanciful."

"Oh." Laxton sounded relieved.

Away to their right policemen were still moving methodically between the trees, prodding at the undergrowth and the dead leaves. Lorraine and Laxton walked on until they emerged on to the bank and, as if by tacit consent, turned left away from the summer-house. There was nobody in sight now.

"What do you want to talk to me about?" Lorraine enquired.

For a moment it seemed that Laxton had changed his mind, he eyed her uncertainly and didn't answer. But perhaps he was only thinking of something else, for he blurted out suddenly, "You're still a beautiful woman, Lorrie."

"Am I?" She smiled. "I spend an awful lot of time and money trying to stay that way."

"I wonder what would have happened if you hadn't gone off to America?"

"I don't know. I guess things would have turned out just about the way they have."

"Perhaps." Laxton looked at her. "Are you happy?"

Lorraine thought for a moment, then she said, "I guess so. I've learnt it's better not to expect too much. Maybe that's a coward's way, but you end up happier. Sometimes I think I'd like to be married now I'm the age I am. Then

I remember the bad times as well as the good and I think maybe it's best the way it is."

"You'll go back to the States?" Laxton asked.

"I expect I will. That's where my work is."

"I've thought about retiring lately. The trouble is, I don't know what I'd do if I did."

There was a defeated note in Laxton's voice and Lorraine said gently, "You didn't bring me here to talk about what might have been, did you, Charles?"

"No." Again he hesitated. "Do you think what's happened has anything to do with the Randall business?" he asked.

"It looks that way."

"But that was all over and done with nearly thirty years ago, what connection can there be? Susan killed Nigel—"

"You really believe that?"

"Don't you?"

The actress shook her head. "No. I couldn't accept it at the time, and I'm more convinced than ever now she didn't. Miles didn't believe it either; that's why he got us all here. Nor does Alan Craig."

"Him!"

"Don't sell him short, Charles. He's nobody's fool."

Laxton scuffed the turf with the toe of his right shoe in a surprisingly schoolboyish gesture. It left a yellow mark on the grass. "Elizabeth's paying him to find out what Jordan was up to."

Lorraine looked mildly startled. "Why? It wasn't anything to do with you."

"How do you know that?" Laxton asked her.

Lorraine didn't answer. Instead she asked, "What do you remember about that weekend?"

"Us mostly. And Phillipson coming to tell us what had happened." The MP paused. "Have you any idea what Jordan was going to do?"

"Only that it must have been something to do with how Nigel died—and we were together then, neither of us killed him." Lorraine hesitated. "Charles, do you know who Miles was?"

"What do you mean, who he was?"

"He was Nigel and Susan's son."

Laxton stopped and stared at Lorraine. "You're sure?"

"Yes. He'd found something that proved Susan didn't shoot Nigel and he intended making a programme about the whole case. You realize if he was killed because he'd learnt who

173

really did it, who it must have been, don't you?"

Ex-Detective Superintendent Levine had once been a burly man. Now, at 82, he seemed to have shrunk inside his skin so that it hung slack, too loose for his frame. But old though he might be, Craig thought, his wits were still sharp and the eyes that peered out from under his shaggy brows still shrewd. He wore glasses for reading, otherwise there wasn't much wrong with his sight.

The two men were sitting in the front room of the cottage Levine and his wife had bought in a village not far from Sudbury when he retired. Mrs. Levine was making tea for them both in the kitchen; Tom Levine didn't hold with newfangled ideas like coffee during the day, tea and beer were coppers' drinks. It was a small, rather gloomy room, spotlessly clean and a little shabby. As if the couple had decided that at their age there was no point in replacing things they might not want much longer. Or perhaps, Craig thought, they merely clung to old, familiar possessions.

"He wasn't a bad lad, Bob Granger," Levine commented. His speech was touched with the

Suffolk accent he had never lost during his many years away from his native county.

Craig guessed that for him "not a bad lad" constituted high praise; Levine didn't give him the impression of a man who sold his compliments cheaply. He suspected, too, that a few years ago the old man would have sent him packing without telling him anything, but now he had reached an age when he couldn't resist the temptation to reminisce.

"You remember the case?" he asked, encouraging him gently.

Tom Levine nodded, smiling a trifle grimly. "Well enough. We didn't have that many murders in those days."

"No," Craig agreed. "Do you remember the Randalls' son? He was only five then."

"There was a little boy. I didn't see much of him; there wasn't any need and his uncle and aunt came and took him away the day after the murder."

"He was Miles Jordan."

"The fellow who's on television?"

"Yes. His uncle and aunt adopted him and changed his name to theirs. He called himself Miles later."

"Can't say I care for his programme," Levine

said. "I dare say it's clever and all that but . . ."

"He's dead," Craig told him. "Somebody shot him yesterday—in the summerhouse where his father was killed."

A dozen years seemed to slip off the old man's back as he demanded, "Where do you come into it?"

"I was staying in the house and I've been hired to make some inquiries about another matter."

"Huh." The grunt was so noncommittal it might equally well have signified disgust or curiosity. "And Bob Granger's in charge?"

"Yes."

"He won't like you getting under his feet."

"I'll do my best not to," Craig said. He paused and crossed his legs the other way to give the old man a few seconds longer to adjust to what he now knew. "The two murders have to be connected. Jordan had invited three of the people who were there when his father was shot and a fourth whose parents were. He set it all up. We were at school together and he asked me there for the weekend. I want to know why."

"Why have you come to me?" Levine enquired.

"Did you ever have any doubt that Susan Randall shot her husband?" Craig asked him.

The old man didn't answer immediately and he was afraid he had taken offence and wouldn't say any more. But there was nothing arrogant or petty about Levine, he knew as well as anyone he wasn't infallible and never had been.

"I was as sure as I could be," he replied slowly. "Most times you know, whether you can prove it or not. She didn't seem the sort. Not that that means anything, I was in the Force long enough to know that."

"She was reprieved." Craig knew it was small consolation to offer the old man for the fear that he might have made a mistake which was beginning to gnaw at his mind. Innocent or not, Susan Randall had endured the torment of waiting for the jury's verdict, hearing herself sentenced to death and weeks in the condemned cell before, finally, dying still in prison. And she had never seen her son again.

Craig knew, too, that it wasn't Levine's fault. If he had believed her to be guilty, so had the DPP, prosecuting counsel, the judge and the jury. Possibly even her own lawyers. She had been convicted on the evidence available to the court, but had Levine taken the easy way and ignored anything which didn't fit in with his belief in her guilt? Craig was convinced he hadn't. After all, what evidence was there that she hadn't murdered her husband? Only her son's apparent certainty—and surely Jordan couldn't have known, he simply wasn't prepared to face the possibility of her guilt— and the doubt of a handful of people who had been her friends. Plus, perhaps, a niggling uncertainty in Tom Levine's mind. It was little enough. And yet . . .

"There wasn't anybody else could have done it," the old man said. "What they did after we'd arrested her wasn't our business."

Craig debated whether to tell him that this morning he had talked to the country vicar who had been the chaplain at the prison where Susan Randall died. The Reverend Peter Wells, too, was an old man now, and possibly readier to talk than he might have been ten years ago, disregarding the constraints of the Official Secrets Act when he saw no harm and perhaps some good coming from it.

Craig decided there was no point in telling Levine that. "You were satisfied no one else could have shot Randall?" he persisted instead, careful not to lead the old man.

178

Levine nodded. "Two of them were in the house, two of them together in the wood, and the rest were playing tennis. The Batemans, the ones in the wood, they hadn't any motive."

"What about the two in the house, Lorraine Maxwell and Laxton? Couldn't one have lied to shield the other?"

Levine grinned. "They were there all right, the maid saw them. She didn't want to tell us at first. Afraid she'd get into trouble. She went into Miss Maxwell's room to do something and found them in bed there. She slipped out again without them seeing her."

Which settled that, Craig thought. "There was an actress staying there that weekend," he remarked. "Not Lorraine Maxwell, a girl named Mary Whittaker. Do you remember her?"

The old man searched in his memory. "Was she the pretty fair one? I didn't care for her. Wouldn't have trusted her an inch; there was something sly about her. But she couldn't have done it, she was playing tennis with three of the others."

Craig nodded, and a moment later Mrs. Levine came in with their tea and a large home made fruit cake. No more was said about the murder.

When he had drunk his tea, eaten a large slice of cake and thanked both the old people, Craig said goodbye and left. He might not have learnt much new, but he wasn't dissatisfied with the fruits of his journey. Tom Levine had confirmed several things he had guessed or suspected.

Gabriella was stretched out on a sun lounger beside the pool, her scanty green swimsuit showing off her tan and the generous curves of her figure. She looked, Gail thought, rather like a self-satisfied cat. At any moment her tongue would flick out and caress her full, sulky lips.

Gabriella hadn't heard her approaching, and the first she knew of the blonde girl standing only a few feet away watching her was when Gail moved and her shadow fell across Gabriella's face. Then she looked up.

"Oh, it's you," she said insolently.

"Yes," Gail agreed. "Where's Simon?"

Gabriella shrugged as well as she could half lying on her back. "I don't know."

"You don't mind being alone?"

Behind her big sun glasses a wary look came

into the dark girl's eyes. "Why should I?" she demanded.

"Because you know something," Gail replied.

"What makes you think I do?"

"I'm sure of it. What is it you know, Gabriella?"

Gail's tone had changed, it was harder now, and suddenly Gabriella was afraid.

"I don't know anything," she said nervously. "I don't."

"I don't believe you," Gail told her.

11

"HAVE you seen Gabriella?"

Simon Fenn was looking for his wife. It wasn't so much that he wanted her, even for Gabriella she was being impossibly trying this weekend with her pretence that she and Jordan had been enjoying some mutual grand passion and, since nobody seemed to take her claim seriously, her sly hints to him that she knew something about Jordan's death. What, she hadn't told him, and he was inclined to believe she was making it up to satisfy her vanity, but the fear that she might haunted him.

Elizabeth Laxton retreated ever so slightly into herself. She had little use for writers—books were all right in their place, but if one lived a properly busy life it was a very minor one—and even less for Fenn whom she regarded as far too emotional and moody. Well bred people concealed their feelings, and he patently was not well bred. On the whole she preferred the policeman, Craig. He might be uncouth, but at least he didn't flaunt his feelings as Fenn did. All the same, what on earth had possessed Miles Jordan when he invited him? Elizabeth wished devoutly that she and Charles hadn't come for this dreadful weekend. Her views on murder were very similar to those of Lady Bracknell on losing one's parents, and she dreaded to think what Charles' constituents would say when they learnt he had been present —well, too nearly present—not at one murder, but at two.

"The last time I saw her she was going towards the swimming pool," she replied with a carefully calculated coolness.

Simon frowned. He knew his wife's addiction to lying stretched out like a giant cod on a fishmonger's slab owed less to her love of the sun than to her conviction that she was irresistibly lovely in a bikini. To men, at least. Gabriella wasn't interested in what women thought. Stupid, unfaithful cow! he thought. There were times when he could cheerfully strangle her.

Who had she set her sights on now? It couldn't be that pompous old fool Laxton, surely. At least she liked men who were the right side of middle age. That left only Craig. The idea that something might be starting between his wife and the moronic ex-policeman set the familiar pangs of jealousy stirring in Fenn.

Who was Craig? Fenn hadn't believed for a moment Jordan's explanation that they were old friends. They might have known each other a long time ago, after all Craig had known Jordan's real name was Michael, but it was hard to see them having much in common or being friends. No, that wasn't the real reason for Craig's being here. So what was?

Fenn walked along the verandah and round the corner of the house towards the pool. He could see Gabriella now, lying on her back on the second sun lounger along, her face, shielded by her sun glasses, turned up almost hungrily to the sun. But the sun, obscured by the light cloud which had blown up in the last half hour, was no longer shining and the air was noticeably cooler.

"Gabby!" he called, his tone edged with spite; she hated being called that.

There was no answer. Stupid bitch! he thought. She was asleep.

It was very quiet here, tucked away round the corner of the house. If anyone else had been sun bathing they must have been driven away when the cloud came up. Not that many of them had probably felt like it after what had happened yesterday and with the police everywhere. Such total relaxation seemed unnatural, almost improper in the circumstances.

Fenn walked towards the lounger wondering what had persuaded Gabriella to remain out here so long, she hated the slightest suggestion of cold.

"Look," he began irritably.

It was only then he realized there was something wrong. There was a limpness about Gabriella that was more than mere relaxation. Her face was turned towards where the sun had been, but now he could see it was only like that because a cushion supporting her head was preventing it slipping sideways.

Then he saw something else, a wooden handle protruding from the left cup of her bikini top. The handle of a knife. And where the blade had penetrated the shiny green fabric there was a small dark stain.

"Oh no!" Fenn breathed.

Craig returned to find the police much more in evidence than they had been when he left. Men were entering and leaving the mobile incident room, but most of them seemed to be on the other side of the house, and when he had put his car away in the garage he walked across to see what was going on.

At the end of the verandah his way was blocked by a large uniformed constable. This one was middle-aged and didn't look as if he could be out-manoeuvred as easily as his colleague of the morning. Beyond him Craig could see the familiar, ominous sight of a canvas screen.

"What's happened?" he enquired.

The constable eyed him phlegmatically. "Who are you, sir?"

"Alan Craig. I'm staying here."

"Mr. Craig." The policeman's tone was flat but the name seemed to give him some private satisfaction. Like a very reserved old tom cat savouring the cream, Craig thought. "The Superintendent would like to see you, sir."

"Oh? Where is he?"

"In the house, sir. I think they call it the morning-room."

In the hall Craig met Gail. She looked pale and strained, he thought.

"Where have you been?" she demanded accusingly.

"To see somebody. Why?"

"Don't you know what's happened?"

"I've seen the screens. Who is it?"

"Gabriella. She was lying out by the pool. Simon found her."

"How was she . . . ?" Craig asked quietly.

"She'd been stabbed. Oh, it's horrible." Gail shuddered.

"Do they know when it happened?"

"I don't think so. He found her about four; we don't know how long she'd been dead." After a moment Gail said more firmly, "We hadn't seen much of the police today, now they're everywhere. The Superintendent was nearly climbing up the wall when he found you weren't here."

"Well, he can come down again now, I'm back."

The morning-room door opened and Granger's burly frame appeared there. "Craig," he said like a man who has been tried to the limits of his endurance.

"Hallo, Super. One of your men said you wanted to see me," Craig told him.

"He was right."

"See you later," Craig said to Gail.

Granger went back into the morning-room,

leaving Craig to follow him, and sat down heavily behind the table. The windows were closed and the room was oppressively hot. Craig could hear a motor coming up the drive and wondered if it was another police car or a hearse.

"I gave instructions I didn't want anybody leaving here," the Superintendent said, making no attempt to conceal his anger.

"I know," Craig agreed.

"But you still went."

"Yes." Craig had been prepared for the CID man's wrath and it didn't intimidate him. On the other hand, he didn't make the mistake of taking it for a sign of weakness.

"Where did you go?" Apparently Granger had abandoned any idea of seeking Craig's co-operation, his manner was as hostile now as it had been when he learnt the other man was an ex-copper.

"To see some people," Craig told him.

There was a brief, uneasy silence.

"That's all you're going to tell me?" Granger rasped.

"One of them was the Vicar of Hesfield. He was the chaplain at the prison where Susan

Randall died. Then I went up to Suffolk to see Tom Levine."

Granger looked as if he couldn't believe it. "What the hell were you doing going to see them?" he demanded.

"I've been hired to make some inquiries," Craig said simply. "It's my job. I thought they might be able to help."

"What inquiries?"

Craig shook his head. "If I find out anything you ought to know, I'll tell you."

"I asked you, what inquiries?" Granger was ominously calm now.

"And I said, I won't hold back anything you should know."

"I'll decide what I should know."

Craig grinned. "You think I may find out something you don't?" he asked.

This time the silence lasted a good deal longer. When he spoke again the Superintendent's manner had changed and in an almost conversational tone he asked, "And were they?"

"Were they what?"

"Able to help."

Craig allowed himself to relax very slightly. He knew that Granger had decided he was likely to learn more by assuming a manner of sweet reasonableness, however much it hurt him. Antagonising him was a risky game and although for the moment the danger point had passed, there could easily be another. Nevertheless, he couldn't afford to let the CID man steamroller him.

"In a negative sort of way," he said.

"And what's that supposed to mean?"

"I asked them if they were completely satisfied Susan Randall killed her husband."

The bemused look returned to Granger's eyes. "You did that? To Tom Levine? What did he say?"

"That it had to be her because there wasn't anybody else."

"Right." Granger sounded gratified. "If everything else is impossible you have to accept what's left, however unlikely it seems."

Craig wondered which of the many courses he must have attended during his long service had implanted that pearl of wisdom in the Superintendent's mind. "And if you can show everything else isn't impossible?" he asked.

"What?"

"The Vicar was convinced she didn't kill Randall. He had known her pretty well for more than two years, and she knew she was dying. Almost the last thing she said to him was that she didn't do it."

"Parsons hate to admit they've been conned," Granger commented in a dismissive tone.

"So do most people," Craig argued. "But I don't think it was that. Only one person I've spoken to who knew her really thinks she was guilty."

"Me."

"I wasn't counting you, you didn't know her. When Levine said he was going to arrest her, you took her guilt for granted."

Granger could still remember the unhappy sense of shock he had felt when they took her away. He hadn't wanted to believe she was guilty—nor think about what would probably happen to her. But over the years he had become less susceptible and more confident that the obvious was usually the truth. He was slightly ashamed of the regret he had felt then. Some people called it growing old, he called it experience.

"Who's the other?" he demanded.

"Caroline Rogers."

"You're telling me that's significant?"

"I don't know," Craig admitted. "It could be. It's interesting, anyway; I wouldn't have thought she was what you'd call perceptive, would you?" He paused. "What time was Gabriella Fenn killed?"

"Between 3.20 and 3.45." Granger eyed him thoughtfully. "Why?"

"I was on my way back from Suffolk then," Craig answered. He knew the CID man would check on that, but he hadn't left the Levines until nearly three, and it would have been impossible for anyone to drive from their house to here in less than two hours. He wondered if Granger considered him seriously as a suspect.

"Mrs. Laxton saw her going towards the pool soon after three," the Superintendent said. "Miss Lakeland says she spoke to her there about half-past. Fenn found her just after 4.15. Or so he claims. According to the doctor, she'd been dead at least half an hour then."

"You don't believe Fenn?" Craig asked.

"I don't believe or disbelieve him. They'd had a row; Mrs. Jordan heard them. It seems his wife had been having an affair with Jordan and more or less taunted him with it."

"She did that all right," Craig agreed. "And there's something else."

"What's that?"

"They'd stayed here before. Gail Lakeland

probably had too. Any of them could have known where Granger kept his gun. The trouble is, none of them was here in 1954."

"Fenn's parents were."

"Yes."

Almost casually Granger remarked, "We've found the gun." Craig's pulses began to beat a little faster. "Where?" he asked.

"In the river about fifty yards upstream from the summerhouse." Granger regarded his companion curiously. "You think the spot's important?"

"I don't know," Craig admitted. "But I don't think Fenn killed his wife."

"Why not?"

"Because Gabriella knew who shot Jordan. She as good as told me so. I'd say she was stupid enough to let whoever it was see she knew—she may even have tried a little quiet blackmail—and that's why she was killed."

"And if it was Fenn killed Jordan?"

"She said it wasn't, that he wouldn't have had the bottle. I asked her who did then, and she wouldn't tell me. I warned her to pass on anything she knew to you and that she was asking for trouble if she didn't."

"She didn't—and she got her trouble,"

Granger commented sombrely. "She could have said that about Fenn to protect him."

Craig shook his head. "Gabriella? You didn't know her, she didn't have exactly a subtle mind. No, she saw something yesterday afternoon all right. Or heard something."

"Even if Fenn didn't kill Jordan, he may still have stabbed her," Granger argued.

Craig regarded him ironically. "You're saying there've been three different murderers?" he asked. "Susan Randall, whoever shot Jordan, and Fenn?"

The Superintendent studied him in silence, then said grudgingly, "All right, let's say Susan Randall was innocent. That leaves us with two."

"One," Craig told him. "Gabriella knew Fenn better than anyone, and if she said he hadn't the bottle to kill Jordan in the summerhouse when there wasn't anybody within a hundred yards, she was probably right. It took a damned sight more nerve to walk up to Gabriella and stab her only twenty or thirty yards from the house with people sitting on the verandah just round the corner. Why didn't she call out?"

"He put his hand over her mouth," Granger

replied. "Her lipstick was smudged. And some-body had locked the French windows on that side of the house so that nobody was likely to go out that way. The curtains were drawn because of the sun."

"He?" Craig repeated. "You're sure it was a man?"

Granger hesitated. "This is between these four walls," he said grimly. "About ten to four, she isn't sure of the exact time, Miss Maxwell walked to the end of the verandah. She saw Mrs. Fenn lying on the lounger thing and turned back. She thinks that as she did so she caught a glimpse of a man in the trees on the other side of the pool, walking away."

"She's sure it was a man?"

"She's not sure about any of it, but she thinks it was a man in a dark suit and wearing a hat."

"I was driving back from Suffolk," Craig observed. "That leaves Laxton, Fenn and Willy Davies."

"And you say it wasn't Fenn."

"I said I didn't think he killed his wife or Jordan, it could have been him Miss Maxwell saw. Where was everybody when Gabriella was stabbed?"

"Miss Lakeland and Fenn say they were in their rooms changing; they'd been playing tennis. The Laxtons were on the lawn, Miss Maxwell on the verandah and Mrs. Jordan in the kitchen."

"What about Caroline Rogers?" Craig enquired.

"It seems she'd been with Miss Maxwell, but she left her and went up to her room to lie down. The Davieses say they were in their flat over the garage."

Any of them could have committed the murder, Craig thought. Probably most of them had seen each other on and off, but it wouldn't have taken more than a minute or two to walk across to where Gabriella was lying, come up behind her, clap a hand over her mouth and stab her. She would have died almost immediately.

Everything indicated that the crime had been carefully planned. His room was the only one which overlooked the pool, and everybody in the house knew he had left early that morning and not returned. The murderer had done all he, or she, could to reduce the chances of being seen but, all the same, he had taken a considerable risk. Whoever it was possessed strong nerves.

"I still think Mrs. Randall killed her husband," Granger declared with the slightly desperate manner of a man clinging to a belief he feels is drifting away from him. If he had to reopen the Randall case his life would become well nigh impossible.

"If she did," Craig pointed out, "Jordan's murder can't have had anything to do with it. So why did he invite all these people? It can't be just coincidence that they nearly all have a direct connection with the Randall murder. And Micky admitted he was up to something. He said he was going to the summerhouse to do some work, and when he was killed the paper in his typewriter was taken. What more do you want?"

Granger knew he was beaten. Right from the beginning he had had a premonition that this wasn't going to be one of those cases you tied up neatly within a couple of days, and he had been right. What had he done to deserve this mess within four months of retiring?

"Have you any idea what Jordan was after?" he enquired gloomily.

"Not a clue," Craig answered. "He didn't

even tell his girl friend. Did you find anything interesting in the desk in the library?"

"Why?" The Superintendent looked suspicious.

"I'm pretty sure Mrs. Laxton was going through the drawers yesterday evening. When I went in there she was bending over it, and I'm fairly certain I heard a drawer shut. She pretended she'd been looking for some writing paper."

"Mrs. Laxton?" Granger sounded horrified.

"Why not? Laxton's scared stiff Jordan had discovered something about him; when he knew I'd been hired to find out what Micky was planning to do he tried to stop me. I'd say our MP's a man with a guilty conscience."

"We didn't find anything there except the usual stuff, receipts and cheque book counterfoils and that."

"Maybe if there is anything it's at his flat. Or his office."

"We'll look there. It could be at his bank."

"Who gets his money?"

"Heaven knows." Granger sounded bitter. "Mrs. Jordan doesn't know, or says she doesn't, and his solicitor's away for the weekend."

"It'll be interesting to see how much he's

left." Craig paused. "Do you want me any more?"

"Not just now. But don't go rushing off again without telling me," the Superintendent added plaintively.

Craig grinned. "I won't," he promised. Halfway to the door he stopped. "Do you remember a girl called Mary Whittaker? A blonde. Actress. She was one of the Randalls' guests."

"No," Granger replied. "Why? What's she got to do with all this?"

"Nothing, as far as I know," Craig assured him. "Tom Levine didn't like her. He said he wouldn't have trusted her an inch."

He went out. The hall was deserted. His conscience was troubling him. Yesterday evening Gabriella had as good as told him she knew something about Jordan's death. True, he had advised her to tell Granger and warned her she was asking for trouble if she didn't, but that was all he had done. If he had pressed her harder, even gone to Granger himself, she might be alive now—and, perhaps, the case would be solved. Instead she had chosen to keep her knowledge to herself. Why?

Craig could think of only two reasons.

Maybe, he thought, he had failed Micky Jordan too. Had Micky known he was in danger and relied on him? There seemed no other reason for his inviting him this weekend.

12

SIMON FENN was distraught. Craig told himself that either the author was a first rate actor or he was genuinely stricken with grief and horror by his wife's death. It seemed he had already forgotten the way she had flaunted her affair with Jordan in front of other people and broadcast her contempt for him. Perhaps it no longer mattered.

Or had Granger been right and this was the grief of guilt? It would be in keeping with what Craig knew of Fenn's character.

"I won't bother you long," he promised.

Fenn shook his head like a boxer who had taken a hard punch to the jaw. "It doesn't matter," he muttered.

"Where was Gabriella when Micky Jordan was shot?"

"In the wood."

"I know, but whereabouts?"

Fenn looked out of eyes which seemed to have difficulty in focussing and made an effort to drag his thoughts back from wherever they had strayed. "What do you mean whereabouts?"

"Which part of the wood?"

"I don't know."

"Are you sure you don't?" Craig persisted. "It may be important."

Fenn struggled to pull himself together. "She went off," he said. "I got fed up with sitting by the pool and I went to find something I'd left in the car. When I got back she wasn't about, so I went down to the wood to see if she was there. That's when I heard Caroline scream. I went on to the summerhouse and found the women there."

"But not Gabriella?"

"No."

"And you didn't see her at all?"

"Not till later."

"So she didn't go by the middle path," Craig said. "She went the other way, didn't she? By the path that runs along the side of the wood past the tennis court?"

"Yes." Fenn's reply was barely audible.

"And she saw something. What was it?"

"I don't know. She wouldn't tell me."

"But there was something?"

Fenn nodded. "She was pleased with herself

afterwards. No, not pleased exactly, sort of triumphant. I told her if she really knew who'd murdered Jordan it might be dangerous, but she just laughed."

"You've no idea what it was?" Craig asked. "Think."

"Do you imagine I haven't thought?" Fenn looked almost desperate.

Craig believed he was telling the truth, and that Gabriella, relishing the sense of power her knowledge gave her, had allowed somebody to see what she knew. Perhaps, even, had boasted of it or used it in an attempt at blackmail. He wouldn't have put that past her.

"Where were you this afternoon?" he asked.

"Playing tennis with Gail. I'd been trying to read but I couldn't concentrate. Gail was looking for you, but you hadn't come back so she asked me. We had three sets, then we came in and I had a shower." The author's expression changed and he regarded Craig suspiciously. "Where were you?"

"Coming back from Suffolk. I had to go and see some people."

The moment's suspicion had lent Fenn some sort of inner strength, now he visibly sagged. "When I changed I went to look for Gabriella," he said. "Elizabeth Laxton told me she'd seen her going towards the swimming pool so I went there. I can't stand that woman, she either looks at you as if you were dirt or she's just too gracious for words. What's she got to be so condescending about?"

Craig grinned. He suspected that, consciously or subconsciously, Fenn was baulking at talking about what he had found. He couldn't blame him for that. "How long did it take you to shower and change?" he enquired.

"I don't know. About twenty minutes, I suppose. It could have been a bit longer. Why?"

Craig ignored the question. "Do you know what Gail did when she came indoors?"

"She said she was going to have a shower too," Fenn answered.

Craig reflected that almost certainly his wife had been murdered while he and Gail were playing tennis. Which would seem to give them both alibis.

"Did your parents ever talk about Randall's murder?" he asked.

Fenn nodded dully. "Once or twice. They're all connected, aren't they? Randall, Jordan, and now Gabriella."

"It looks like it," Craig agreed. "Did they say anything to suggest they thought Susan Randall was innocent?"

"Only that they couldn't believe she'd done it. But people often say that, don't they?"

"Sometimes," Craig agreed. "It's better than saying 'I knew all the time it was her.'"

It didn't make any real difference, he thought, it just added two more to the list of those who had known Susan Randall and couldn't see her killing her husband. Perhaps their reaction was mostly emotional, but he had other grounds for thinking she was innocent. And still, if you excepted Granger, there was only one person who insisted on her guilt.

"Thanks," he said.

He was at the door when Fenn said suddenly, "All I know is that it was something about Gail."

Startled, Craig asked, "What was?"

"What Gabriella knew."

"You're sure?"

"Well, something she said . . ."

Craig left him and went downstairs to the drawing-room. Sandra and the other guests were there, looking as if they were waiting for something to happen and fearful what it might

205

be. When he came in they watched as he walked across to an empty chair next to Gail. She gave him a nervous smile, but he sensed the hostility in some of the others and knew they still regarded him as in some obscure way being on "the other side". It was absurd when all of them, save perhaps one, must be desperately anxious for the murderer to be arrested as soon as possible, but people's reactions in the face of a crisis were often illogical. He had the feeling he had experienced when he first arrived, of belonging to a different world from theirs. Perhaps they would like him to be the murderer.

"I guess you've heard what's happened?" Lorraine asked him.

Her accent was more pronounced and Craig wondered if, consciously or unconsciously, she was exaggerating it as if to say she was a stranger; only just arrived in Britain, she couldn't have a motive for killing Jordan. But that didn't stand up, it was unlikely the murderer had had a motive until he arrived here. Possibly not until the discussion at breakfast yesterday. Had Micky put the emphasis on "you" when he told Fenn he had nothing to worry about, suggesting somebody else had?

Actresses, especially Hollywood stars, had to be pretty tough, even ruthless, to reach the top and stay there for years. Under her charm and friendliness, was Lorraine really as hard as nails?

And Charles Laxton? It wasn't hard to believe that behind the public face he was selfish enough to kill to protect himself. Easier still to see his wife planning and committing a murder, there was a steely quality about Elizabeth. Moreover she was a shrewd, clever woman, and very likely one who would go to almost any lengths to protect her husband and his position. Position meant a great deal to women like her.

It meant less to the Caroline Rogers of this world. They were snobs, but their own wellbeing took precedence over everything. Like cats, they valued their creature comforts very highly.

"Yes," Craig said, answering Lorraine's question.

"Of course, you and the police—" Caroline began spitefully.

Gail interrupted her. "I told him."

"Oh, I see."

Craig suspected Caroline had deliberately

invested her remark with a significance it didn't possess, and he was surprised to see that Gail had flushed.

"The police have found the gun," Laxton announced with the air of a man who finds a silence oppressive and has to say something to break it.

The others carefully avoided looking at him.

"So I heard," Craig said.

A few minutes later, when Mrs. Davies came in to speak to Sandra, he saw the housekeeper had been crying.

It was past nine when he crossed the yard, climbed the outside staircase, and rang the bell of the Davieses' flat. From inside he could hear the sounds of an argument, the gardener's voice raised angrily, then his wife's.

When the bell rang they stopped abruptly and Willy Davies came to the door wearing an open necked shirt, faded jeans and sandals. In contrast to his chirpiness when Craig encountered him in the wood, he looked wary and suspicious.

"What is it?" he demanded.

"Can you spare me a minute or two?" Craig asked.

"Why? This is my flat and it's Sunday evening, aren't I entitled to any time off then?"

"About as much as I am," Craig told him equably.

The little man's wariness became more marked. "I knew it," he said disgustedly. "You are a ruddy copper."

"No."

Mrs. Davies appeared at her husband's shoulder. "Oh, it's you, Mr. Craig," she said. The sight of him seemed to come as a relief to her and Craig wondered if she had expected the police back again. "Can we help you?"

"I don't know," he admitted. "Could I come in?"

"Let the gentleman in, Willy," Mrs. Davies told her husband.

The Welshman hesitated, then stood aside reluctantly and Craig followed him into a comfortable, airy living-room extending the whole depth of the building.

"What do you want then?" Davies demanded, seating himself in an easy chair so large it almost engulfed him.

"Willy," his wife chided him. "Do sit down, Mr. Craig."

She seated herself on an upright chair near

her husband and Craig took one end of the settee where he was facing them both.

"I've nothing to do with the police," he said. "I work for myself and I've been asked to make some inquiries about something Mr. Jordan was working on. It can't hurt him, but if you don't want to tell me anything, that's up to you."

"I dare say another question or two won't make much difference," the gardener said bitterly.

"The police have been asking a lot?" Craig sounded sympathetic.

"You'd expect them to, wouldn't you?" Mrs. Davies said reasonably. "After all, it was Willy's gun they took, whoever it was."

"Don't you start again, Joan," the Welshman told her. "I've 'ad enough of it these last two days, I tell you."

"When did you last see your gun?" Craig asked.

"Yesterday morning. After I'd been out shooting those damned pigeons. I came back 'ere and put it away just like I always did."

"Where was that?"

Willy Davies was too aggrieved to reflect that Craig's questions were almost the same as those the police had asked, and seemed to have little to do with his employer's work. "In the cupboard in the old tack room," he replied.

"Did many people know you kept it there?"

"How would I know? Mrs. Jordan did—and that MP fellow had been nosing around. Said he was interested in cars. Any of them might have known, it wasn't a secret then."

"I knew," Mrs. Davies said.

"Don't be daft," her husband told her.

"Miss Lakeland and the Fenns had stayed here before, hadn't they?" Craig enquired.

"Yes." Mrs. Davies nodded. "Miss Lakeland had been twice and Mr. and Mrs. Fenn were here about two months ago."

"But none of the others?"

"No."

The flat faced south-east and the sun was low in the west, but neither of the Davieses made a move to switch on a light. Through the open window Craig could hear occasional footsteps outside as Granger's men entered and left the caravan. He was conscious of a mild sense of deprivation because he didn't know what the police were doing or how much progress they had made.

"Did Mr. Jordan tell you anything about this weekend?" he asked.

"All we knew was who was coming," Mrs. Davies replied. "And then when he rang to say he'd been held up in London and wouldn't be here until just before dinner."

Craig was beginning to wonder if that had been a deliberate ploy; Micky had wanted the three guests who had been here when Randall was murdered to experience alone the shock of realizing they were again guests in the Randalls' house. And it had been a shock, to one of them at least. For the same reason he hadn't invited any of them here before. Which suggested they were the only guests who really mattered to him, and the rest were only extras to fill out the cast. Cast, Craig thought, was the right word.

"How did you get on with him?" he asked, his manner still relaxed. He didn't want to alarm the gardener and his wife. "What sort of man was he? I'd only seen him once since I left school."

"He was all right then," Willy Davies said firmly. "I don't care what people say, man, he was very good to us."

"Oh, he was kind to us," his wife agreed. It struck Craig she was a good deal less enthusiastic than her husband.

"You didn't care for him?" he suggested.

She gave the slightest of shrugs. "It didn't make any difference if we liked him or not, he treated us very fair."

"When you're in trouble you learn who your friends are," Willy said. It might be a cliché, clearly he meant it.

"Would you say he was a cruel man?"

Willy looked puzzled but Mrs. Davies said enigmatically, "It depends what you mean by cruel. You can hurt people without knocking them about, can't you?"

"Somebody said he was."

"There are some people always looking for faults in others," the gardener proclaimed angrily. "Cast out the mote in thine own eye."

Craig regarded him with interest. The little Welshman reminded him of a fundamentalist preacher he had listened to on quiet Sundays when he was a young copper on the beat. "Mrs. Jordan seems all right," he remarked.

"She is." A new warmth had crept into Mrs. Davies's voice.

"She betrayed him," her husband declared.

"You won't find me blaming her for that. Not after what she had to put up with. Miss Lakeland's a nice girl, but . . . Well, it's no wonder Mrs. Jordan had had enough of it. And

213

Mr. Newton's all right, he'll look after her even if he hasn't two pennies to rub together. It's good to see her looking so happy. Or it was until this happened." Mrs. Davies stopped. "Oh well, it's no concern of mine."

"She'll have enough for both of them now, I expect," Craig observed.

"I wouldn't know about that." Mrs. Davies's tone suggested she was afraid she had gone too far.

"There's a lot you don't know," her husband told her witheringly.

Craig suspected they were taking up an argument which had begun before his arrival and which he had interrupted. "Did you hear those planes go over yesterday afternoon?" he asked the housekeeper.

She nodded. "Beastly noisy things. I said so to Mrs. Jordan when she came."

"Of course, she was with you, wasn't she?"

"She came to the window and asked where Mr. Jordan was. I told her in the summerhouse and she went to find him."

"Well, thank you both," Craig said, standing up.

Mrs. Davies went to the door with him. Stepping outside on to the tiny landing she drew the door to behind her. "The police are trying to make out Willy killed Mr. Jordan," she said bitterly. "Just because whoever it was used his gun, and because of something that happened years ago. He thought the world of him, he wouldn't have dreamed of doing him any harm. Anyway," she added defiantly, "he was with me all the afternoon."

She would maintain that, true or not, until Kingdom Come, Craig thought. Not that he believed Davies had shot Jordan; apart from anything else the Welshman had no connection with what had happened in 1954. Also, the murder showed all the signs of careful planning and if he ever killed anyone, Craig was pretty sure, it would be on the spur of the moment in a fit of ungovernable rage.

Nevertheless he was convinced Mrs. Davies was lying. For one thing, Sandra had said nothing about their being together when she asked where Micky was.

"Did you ever hear Mr. Jordan mention a girl named Mary Whittaker?" he asked.

From the woman's blank expression he was convinced she hadn't and the name meant nothing to her. Which was only what he had expected.

"I don't think you need worry too much about the police," he said. "I'd be surprised if they thought either of you had anything to do with it."

Maybe he shouldn't have told her that, he thought as he walked back to the house, but it was true.

Gail was standing on the verandah. "What's happening?" she asked him.

"I don't know," he replied. "The usual routine things, I suppose."

"I tried to read, but I couldn't concentrate. It's as if we're all trapped in a sort of limbo. We don't belong here, any of us—except Sandra—but we can't leave and what's happening may affect us for the rest of our lives."

"You'll soon leave it behind you," Craig told her.

"Will we? I wonder if we'll ever be quite the same again."

"That might not be a bad thing as far as some people I could mention are concerned."

Gail smiled. After a moment she said, "I've been trying to remember what it was like before I met Miles. I know it's not long, but somehow he's been so much a part of everything . . ."

"Yet you say it was all over," Craig reminded her.

"I know. That's what's so strange about it."

"What really made you decide to break it off? I know it's none of my business but I've been trying to find out what Micky was really like."

Gail didn't answer immediately, then she said slowly, "I think he was completely selfish. I don't mean greedy or mean, he could be terribly generous, he simply wasn't interested in anything that didn't affect him or he couldn't use. He didn't pretend to be. At least he was that honest."

Craig knew she was thinking that Jordan hadn't minded slanting a programme to make the point he wanted, however prejudiced that might be, or suppressing evidence if it didn't support his angle.

"When you were with him you hardly noticed it," Gail went on. "He was very good at manipulating people. But lately I hadn't been with him so much and I saw things I hadn't noticed before. Or perhaps I had been aware of them, but tried to pretend they weren't there. I got the feeling he was using me, although I couldn't see how." Gail paused. "If I hadn't broken it off, he would have dropped me soon."

"As bad as that?" Craig asked.

"He wanted all his relationships to remain casual. I don't mean just his relationships with women, like that, everything. I think he was afraid of becoming involved, emotionally or in any other way—and it didn't occur to him that might not be enough for other people. Either that or he didn't care." Gail turned away. "I expect I'm exaggerating. And it was fun while it lasted; I don't bear him any grudges."

The front door opened and Craig saw a woman's figure silhouetted against the light in the hall.

"Oh, there you are," Sandra said lightly, coming towards them. "I saw Gail go out, and when she didn't come back I thought . . . I'm afraid we're all on edge tonight."

She was speaking to Craig. Now she took his other side and together the three of them went back into the house. As Sandra opened the drawing-room door Craig saw the other guests all there and, leaving the two women to join them, he sprinted up the stairs and along the landing to the door of Jordan's room. Pausing to make sure nobody had followed him, he opened it, slipped inside, and walked across to the wardrobe.

Jordan had possessed a good many clothes. Craig concentrated on the jackets, paying particular attention to the sleeves. Then he looked at the top shelf.

When he went downstairs again five minutes later he was frowning.

Everybody seemed reluctant to be the first to go to bed that night. Perhaps, Craig thought, fear was working its insidious way with them and they disliked the prospect of being alone in their rooms. In the end it was Lorraine who made the first move, and, as if she had removed some barrier, the others very soon followed.

Craig didn't get ready for bed at once. Instead he sat in a chair by the open window. Outside the night was very still, without even the lightest breeze to stir the leaves in the copse. The moon was up and pools of shadow lay across the lawn. But he saw none of that, he was immersed in his thoughts.

It seemed clear that Jordan had arranged this party because he intended making a programme about his father's murder and that he had been shot to stop him. Lorraine had suggested he planned to stage a new trial, and Craig believed she was right; it would have been in keeping with what he had heard himself, and what he had learnt about the dead man's character.

Jordan wouldn't have gone to the lengths he had without strong evidence, not only of his mother's innocence, but of who was guilty. Find the murderer of thirty years ago and you had the killer of Jordan himself and Gabriella.

There was only one person that could be. And yet . . .

A small cloud passed across the moon, darkening the shadows on the lawn. A few seconds more and it had gone.

If that person was innocent, there could be no direct connection between Randall's death and the murders this weekend, except the obvious one that some of the guests here now had been staying with the Randalls then, too. From the murderer's point of view that could have been fortuitous. Almost irrelevant. And in that event, Granger had been right and there were two murderers.

At least seven of the people here now might have had a motive for killing Jordan. Sandra would probably inherit her husband's estate; Laxton was clearly frightened Jordan had known something about him, and Elizabeth seemed to Craig capable of killing to protect him; Fenn had had to listen to his wife boasting about her affair with the dead man, and Gabriella herself must have known Jordan no longer cared for her, if he had ever done so. Gail? Cool blondes could be capable of deep passions, and she might have been lying when she said she had been going to tell Micky it was all over between them. Or perhaps she had had another motive. As for Willy Davies, he was unpredictable and very likely violent during his fits of anger. Who could tell what bitterness and hatred he might have been storing up?

Only Caroline and Lorraine seemed to have had no motive apart from Joan Davies, and Craig was inclined to rule her out.

Opportunity was more difficult. Sandra had come from the village and was talking to the housekeeper, and no one appeared to know where Willy was. As far as Craig could tell, Fenn, Caroline, the Laxtons, Gail, Gabriella and Lorraine could all have shot Jordan. Of them Gabriella was dead and Lorraine and Caroline had had no apparent motive. That left Fenn, Gail, the Laxtons, and possibly Willy Davies with both a reason for killing him and the opportunity to do so.

One of them had murdered Gabriella too.

Fenn and Gail claimed they were showering and changing when she was killed, but either of them could have slipped downstairs, out through one of the French windows, stabbed her and returned to the house via the wood. True, Fenn had appeared to be genuinely distressed this evening, but it was not unknown for murderers to show all the signs of remorse after their crimes. Anyway, he could have been acting. As for the others, Sandra said she was in the kitchen, and the rest in different parts of the garden; none of them could prove where he or she was at the crucial time.

Sighing, Craig stood up and started to undress.

13

THE atmosphere was no more relaxed the next morning. At breakfast Sandra and Craig alone seemed at their ease, and even Lorraine appeared preoccupied. Gail and Fenn looked lost, Elizabeth Laxton remote, and her husband, although he did his best to conceal it, was clearly uneasy. Caroline, lost in a nervous apathy, hardly spoke.

When Mrs. Davies came in she looked as if she hadn't slept much. Craig wondered if there had been a scene after he left her and her husband last night.

After breakfast he went out on to the verandah; Granger had again taken over the library. Elizabeth Laxton sought him out there.

"I have decided there is little point now in trying to find out what Miles Jordan was planning to do," she said. If the knowledge that he was aware she had been searching Jordan's desk embarrassed her she showed no sign of it, her manner was as cool and assured as ever. "I don't imagine you have spent much time on it yet, but if you send me your account for whatever you think is due to you I'll pay it."

Craig regarded her with interest. During his time in the police he had met all sorts of people, including women like her, but he couldn't remember one who had possessed quite her degree of unconscious arrogance and self-assurance. She made his hackles rise, and yet, in a perverse way, he couldn't help respecting her.

"It's too late," he said.

Elizabeth's fastidious eyebrows rose just far enough to register surprised distaste. "Too late?" she queried. "I can't see how it can be. I employed you, now I'm cancelling those instructions."

"Okay," Craig told her cheerfully, "I don't work for you. That's all right with me. But you can't stop whatever it is your husband's so anxious to keep secret coming out now."

Elizabeth looked as if she would like to strike him. Instead, after a moment staring at him in angry silence, she turned and stalked back into the house.

Left to himself, Craig wondered if she really believed she could run her part of the world to suit herself. Perhaps she was so used to getting her own way she took it for granted anyone who had the impertinence to oppose her would soon submit. Such ideas could be dangerous.

Soon afterwards the Laxtons left. Clearly they couldn't put The White House behind them quickly enough, and Granger had no justification for insisting they stayed. Craig suspected he wasn't sorry to see them go, he must have found Laxton, with his connections and his ability to stir up trouble discreetly if he felt so inclined, slightly intimidating.

Craig himself was uncertain what to do. The case was no concern of his, and he didn't think the CID man seriously considered him a suspect; there was no reason why he shouldn't return to London and try to pick up the trail of the elusive Hollins. That would at least be good for a few quid, while time he spent here was money down the drain now Elizabeth Laxton was no longer paying him.

And yet, having been so closely involved in the events of the last few days, he was reluctant to leave before the case was resolved. Also, there were still some questions which he wanted answered—for his own satisfaction, if nothing else.

While he was still on the verandah, contemplating the immediate future—and the not so immediate, which didn't look too bright just now—Gail wandered out of the house. She looked unsettled, Craig thought.

"The Laxtons have gone," she said.

"I know."

"I can't make up my mind whether to go or not. I can't wait to get away from here but . . . I don't know, it seems a bit like running away somehow."

"I shouldn't worry about that," Craig told her. "There's nothing you can do, and if Granger wants you for anything he can always find you."

Gail's eyes widened with alarm. "Why should he want me?"

"I didn't say he would, just that if he did he'd know where you were," Craig said reassuringly. "You'll have to let him know where you're going to be."

"Yes." Gail looked out across the lawn and the rosebeds to the gentle slope of the ground towards the road and the village. "It's lovely here, but if I ever came back I'd never be able to like it again, however long it was." She turned to look at him. "What are you going to do, Alan?"

"I don't know. There are one or two things I want to see to here, then I expect I'll go back to London. You never know, there may be some work waiting for me."

Gail laughed. "I'll go and see if Sandra wants a hand with anything."

She went back into the house and Craig started walking towards the stable block. Before he reached it he turned right, following the path round the side of the lawn. Gravel crunched under his feet, but he was as unaware of it as he was of the sun burning his face as he walked on.

Could Granger be right after all and Fenn had killed both Jordan and Gabriella? He had had both motive and opportunity—and probably he was selfish enough, for most murderers put their own interests before everything—while in his defence there was only his wife's almost contemptuous remark that he couldn't have killed Jordan. It wasn't much. Moreover Craig had seen him walking towards the stables only a short time before the murder, and Fenn could well have known where Willy Davies kept his gun. If he had taken it then, he must have come along this path, killed Jordan, and walked on for fifty yards along the bank before throwing the rifle into the stream. And then? Starting back through the wood, he had heard Caroline scream and returned to the summer-house to find the women there.

But why, when every second was vital, had he waited to remove the paper from Jordan's typewriter? As far as Craig could see, his only motive for shooting Jordan was the latter's affair with Gabriella, and whatever Micky had been typing it was unlikely to have anything to do with that. As far as Jordan was concerned their relationship had ended some time before.

No, it was inconceivable that there wasn't a link between his death and what had happened here thirty years ago. Micky had staged this party to show that his mother hadn't shot his father and, it seemed fairly safe to assume, who he thought had. Only Lorraine, Caroline and Charles Laxton of his guests had been staying here then. Had one of them killed Randall? Jordan must have believed so—and possessed evidence to support his belief.

But which of them?

Craig thought he knew that.

He had reached the river. The boat he had seen on Saturday afternoon had gone, and the only signs of life were a few small fish darting about just below the green-brown surface of the water. The boat. Craig gazed at the spot where he had glimpsed it while he was waiting for the police, nosed in to the bank just beyond the ash tree whose branches trailed in the water. It was just the sort of place a young man and a girl might tie up to be alone. And if there had been a couple in the boat then, they might have seen something—or someone—without realizing its significance. A man walking along the bank, for instance.

Had Granger looked into that possibility?

Craig set off along the bank in the opposite direction from the summerhouse, past the corner of the wood and the rhododendrons, until he came to the drive at a point a few yards from where it met the road. There was a small group of men at the gates, laughing and talking amongst themselves and with the solitary policeman on duty there. Some of them had photographers' bags slung from their shoulders. As Craig walked past one or two of them asked who he was and if he had anything to tell them. He grinned, shook his head and walked on towards the village.

At that time on a Monday morning the street was almost deserted. Apart from an old man leading a mongrel terrier on a length of cord, he could see only three elderly women talking outside the butcher's. When he approached they turned their heads to watch him with long unembarrassed stares, exercising the country-woman's right to know as much as possible of what was happening in her village. They didn't know who he was, or even that he had come from The White House, just now any stranger was an object of interest to them.

Crossing the street, he pushed open the door of the post office-cum-general store. Over it there was a sign "H. SMITH, proprietor. Licensed to sell tobacco". As Craig walked in the quiet clang of the old-fashioned bell mounted at the top of the door took him back thirty years to the shop his father had owned then in Ilford. But time had brought changes even in Lower Marking, and H. Smith had done his, or her, best to keep up with them. Where once wellingtons and buckets had hung from the ceiling and a counter had run the width of the shop, now there were two rows of back-to-back shelving reaching from the floor, its bare boards covered with vinyl tiles, nearly to the ceiling. Much of the remaining space was occupied by a freezer cabinet and a check-out point, but at the back of the shop a tiny counter surmounted by a grille served as Lower Marking's post office.

Craig helped himself to a *Daily Express* from the rack just inside the door and looked round. At first he could see nobody, then an elderly face, its soft, plump cheeks topped by white hair so pitifully thin he could see the pink scalp through it, peeped round the end of the grille and asked in a reedy soprano, "Can I help you?"

"I've taken this," Craig said, holding out the paper. "Is that all right?"

"Oh yes, dear."

The owner of the voice slid down off her stool and emerged into the shop. Craig, who had assumed she was sitting on a low stool, was surprised to find she really was well under five feet tall.

"Can I get you anything else?" she enquired, taking the money for the paper. "Are you one of the newspaper gentlemen?"

Craig was about to assure her he wasn't when he realized that a denial would probably provoke further questions and, far from disliking the presence of the Press in her village, she was rather thrilled by it.

231

"Not exactly," he compromised.

"Oh, I see, dear." She gave him a knowing look which puzzled him until he saw she supposed he was from the BBC or ITN.

"I was wondering if there was anywhere in the village I could hire a boat," he said. It was hardly likely a representative of either television network would take time off for boating, but she might credit him with the initiative to enter the White House grounds from the river or, at least, to want a closer look at the summerhouse.

She looked doubtful. "I don't know, dear. People don't seem to go boating like they did when I was a girl. It was lovely, drifting along on a sunny afternoon with someone you liked rowing and the birds singing. I remember . . ." She stopped suddenly and, to Craig's surprise, blushed even pinker. More briskly she added, "The only boat I know round here now's Mr. Lambert's. I've never heard of him hiring it out, but he might, I suppose."

"Mr. Lambert?" Craig asked.

"He lives in the red brick house just across the street there next to Mr. Newton's. Chantry House it's called," the old lady told him.

Craig thanked her and left. The three women were still talking outside the butcher's. He crossed the street, conscious of their gaze following him, passed a 16th century cottage with a sagging roof and stained plaster, and rang the bell at the door of the Queen Anne house next to it.

His ring was answered by a very tall, very thin man in shabby corduroy trousers and a check shirt. His face was lean and his straight fair hair rather long, so that everything about him seemed to be in vertical lines.

"I'm looking for a boat to hire," Craig explained, "and the lady in the post office suggested I ask you."

"Did she?" The thin man looked puzzled, as if the idea of wanting to hire a boat was something completely outside his experience. Or perhaps it was only surprise that Craig should have been sent to him. "I wonder why."

The front door of the next door cottage slammed and, looking past Craig, he said in the tones of a man welcoming a diversion, "'Morning, Tony."

Craig turned and saw a man of twenty-seven or eight with dark hair and strangely gentle features.

"'Morning, Steven," the young man said.

He walked off in the direction of the shops

and Lambert concentrated on Craig and the matter of boats with evident reluctance.

"Sorry," he said, "I'm afraid I can't help. To be honest, I don't know I'd want to hire my old tub out anyway, but as it happens I can't, some kids took it the other day and knocked a hole in it."

Craig experienced a sudden pang of disappointment. "Hard luck," he said sympathetically. "Where did you keep it?"

"Tied up at the bottom of the orchard there." Lambert jerked his head to indicate the back of his house. "It wasn't worth anything; I hardly ever used it."

"When did it happen?"

"Goodness knows. I didn't even know it was gone until the police came to see me yesterday. They'd found the kids playing in it up by the bridge. According to them they'd found it drifting, but I expect they were lying."

"The bridge on the Murtleigh road?" Craig asked, his disappointment fading.

"That's right."

"So that's it then. You don't happen to know of another boat round here I might hire, do you?"

Lambert shook his head. "Mine was the only

one in the village, I'm pretty sure of that. Sorry."

"Well, thanks anyway," Craig said.

He started to walk back. The three women had finished their conversation and were splitting up; as he passed one of them went into the post office. The others' eyes watched him as he walked up the street.

The boat hadn't looked as if it was holed when he saw it on Saturday afternoon, he thought. The odds were it wasn't, if the boys had found it there and worked it the three hundred yards or more down the river to the bridge. Most likely they had tired of it and bombarded it with stones; if the wood was as old as Lambert had hinted, it could well have split.

When he arrived back at The White House, he fetched a notebook from his room and took himself off to the summerhouse without seeing anyone other than two policemen in the distance. Granger's men had finished with the little wooden building and he was fairly confident he wouldn't be disturbed there, he couldn't see any of the guests who remained going near it.

Jordan's typewriter and the thin pile of paper

had been removed, otherwise everything seemed to be just as it had been on Saturday afternoon. Even the table and chair were where they had been then, their wooden surfaces still bearing traces of fingerprint powder. Craig sat on the chair and placed his notebook and a ballpoint pen on the table in front of him.

Micky had been typing when he was shot, when his body was found a few minutes later his hands were still resting on the keys. But there was no paper in the machine. A typewriter wasn't like a piano, nobody sat like that unless they were actually typing. So what had Micky written that was so incriminating that the murderer had removed it?

Tom Levine, a capable and conscientious detective, was convinced no one but Susan Randall could have shot her husband, so what could Jordan have known that made him a threat to one of his guests? Craig believed he knew the answer to that, but proving it after all this time was a different matter. Almost certainly it would be impossible.

He stayed seated at Jordan's table for a long time, while the sun climbed higher in the sky and insects hummed outside the little summerhouse. Occasionally he made a note in his own brand of shorthand, which was unintelligible to other people and occasionally almost so to him. At last he stood up, slipped the book into his pocket, and returned to the house.

But he didn't take the direct path through the middle of the wood. Instead he walked fifty yards along the bank, counting the paces. There was nothing to mark the spot where the murderer had thrown Davies' rifle into the stream, no tree, nothing that marked out that spot from any other along the bank, and he turned away from the river along another path he hadn't seen before, although he had known of its existence. It ran along the side of the wood, and clearly it was little used, for the grass had grown quite long and was seeding. But people had gone that way recently, trampling it flat for much of the way. The other side of the path was marked by a two strand wire fence with, beyond it, a field of wheat already changing colour from gold to brown.

Walking fast, it took Craig one minute fifty-five seconds from the summerhouse to the verandah.

Sandra was alone in the drawing-room. When he walked in she looked up.

"I've come to say goodbye," he told her.

237

"You're going?" There was regret in her voice.

"I have to get back to work." For what? he thought. To read two months old magazines and chat up Georgie? But the prospect wasn't so unattractive, he had had enough of over-developed egos these last few days.

"Yes, of course." Sandra smiled palely. "I'm sorry we couldn't have met when things were different. You'll be glad to get away, won't you? I wish I could go too, just lock up and leave it all."

Craig nodded. "Lorraine's staying?" he asked.

"For a day or two. She said she would if I wanted her to. She's been wonderful."

"I'll go and get my bag," Craig said.

It was several minutes before he came down again, and Sandra was in the hall.

"I'll say goodbye then," he told her. It sounded feeble; he too wished they could have met under different circumstances.

"Goodbye, Alan." Her eyes met his. There was a strange brightness in them, he thought. "Whatever's happened, I'm glad we met."

Craig nodded. Suddenly Sandra put her hands on his shoulders and kissed him.

He didn't know what to say. "Thank you for having me," hardly seemed appropriate, so he settled for "Say goodbye to Gail for me, will you?"

"Yes." Sandra was looking at him as if there was more she wanted to say, but she couldn't find the words. Or wasn't sure enough of him.

He carried his case out to the garage. Granger was in the caravan.

"I'm off," Craig told him.

"All right."

"Will you be here all day?"

"Why?"

"I might ring you."

"If you're not going to co-operate, you needn't bother," Granger said acidly.

"I've told you all I know." Not all I believe, not all I'm convinced is the real truth, but that's not the same thing, Craig told himself. You want facts.

"Thanks," Granger said ironically.

"If I were you, I'd have a look in Jordan's wardrobe. Especially the sleeve of one of the jackets," Craig told him.

The Superintendent eyed him suspiciously. "What for?"

239

"I found something there last night. It's still there this morning. Will you be here?"

"If I'm not, they'll know where to find me."

Craig nodded. Walking across to the garage, he pulled open the doors, threw his case in the back of his car, and climbed into the driving seat. Sandra was right, he thought, he was glad to be leaving. Some of Jordan's bitterness and cruelty had polluted the atmosphere, sullying this lovely place. Pushing in the ignition key, he started the engine and backed the Dolomite out of the garage.

The reporters were still clustered by the gate as he drove past.

Craig parked on a double yellow line, stuck a card with the single word "DOCTOR" printed on it inside his windscreen, and walked round the corner to his office.

"Coo, you've 'ad a weekend and an 'arf," Georgie greeted him. "It's in the pipers."

Craig regarded her critically. Since he saw her last on Friday her long dark hair had become a tousled mass of red-brown curls.

"I don't like it," he said.

"'Oo asked you if you did?" Georgie countered, affronted. "I din't 'ave it done for your benefit." Then in a different tone she added, "Don't you really?"

Craig grinned. "I expect I'll get used to it."

Georgie brightened. "I said you'd be sorry if you didn't go, din't I?"

"You were wrong," Craig told her. He would give a lot to go back to Friday and wipe out all that had happened since. To spend the weekend as usual, doing nothing in particular, maybe having one or two jars with a few friends on Saturday evening. To turn the clock back and start again like one of the characters in the time plays that chap Priestley wrote. Craig had once seen an amateur production of *Dangerous Corner*.

Looking back, his clearest memories of the last two days all seemed to include Sandra. Her arrival when he and the three women were waiting for the police on the bank, her courage when he talked to her later, their walk in the dusk, and the look in her eyes when they said goodbye this morning. Micky, he thought, you were a damned fool. You didn't know when you were well off.

"What was Lorraine Maxwell like?" Georgie demanded.

"All right," Craig answered.

"You can't say somebody like that's just orl right!"

"Okay, she still isn't bad to look at, she's a bit showy, but I liked her. Like I said, she's all right."

"Oh you!" Georgie snorted.

"Have there been any customers?"

"What d'you think? And Les said remind you the rent's due Friday. D'you want some coffee?"

"Please, Georgie. And you can tell Les his rent's safe; if I was thrown out of here I wouldn't have anyone to bring me coffee."

"Just as long as you remember," Georgie said.

Craig went into his office, saw there was no post and switched on his answering machine. There was nothing on that either, and he picked up the E—K telephone directory, flipping through the pages until he found the number of Jordan's office in the West End.

It took several minutes and he spoke to three people before he was finally put through to Jordan's personal assistant. They must be in quite a state there today, he thought; the drawbridges were up and they were repelling all boarders. But Judith Cromer sounded as cool and in control as when he had spoken to her before. To his surprise, she agreed to have lunch with him.

He told himself she was probably much older than she sounded and about as attractive as the back of a bus; you couldn't expect girls who accepted invitations from strangers at such short notice to be good looking too. Life wasn't that kind.

Replacing the phone, he looked up another number. Max Dooley was the journalist he had asked for information about Micky Jordan after the latter's call on him. His path and Craig's had first crossed some years before when Craig was a very junior member of a team investigating an armed robbery and Dooley a crime reporter on another paper. Since then they had met several times and got to know each other fairly well. Well enough for Craig to feel no compunction about asking the journalist for information again.

He glanced at his watch. It was nearly twelve. Any time now Dooley would depart to the pub for lunch with some of his cronies. When he returned, mellow but still sober, would be a better time to ask a favour of him.

"Now?" he wanted to know when Craig asked if he could come to see him.

"No. How about half-three this afternoon?" Dooley's lunch "hours" were inclined to be elastic.

"Okay." Dooley couldn't see there was likely to be anything in it for him, but if Craig wanted to pick his brains he didn't mind. The poor sod probably needed all the help he could get just now.

"Thanks," Craig said. He was putting the phone down when Georgie came in with his coffee. "Sorry, I've got to go out," he told her.

"You've only just come in."

"I know. I'll be back by four." Craig gulped some of the coffee. "Strewth, it's scalding!"

"If you ask me," Georgie told him, "it's not good for you, all this dashing abaht."

Oh no! Craig told himself. She was getting maternal. If this went on, he would have to look out.

"Not at your age," Georgie added coolly, picking up the cup and saucer and heading for the door.

Craig threw a magazine at her retreating back and missed.

14

JUDITH CROMER was waiting for him in the foyer of the big concrete and glass block where Jordan had his offices. Craig's fears weren't realized, she was in her late twenties, auburn haired, slim and extremely attractive; her clothes and her make-up were impeccable. Nor did she seem mercenary, it was her suggestion that they should lunch at an unpretentious little Italian restaurant just round the corner.

"I heard about it Saturday evening. Sandra phoned me," she said when the waiter had taken their order and departed.

"Had you worked for Jordan long?" Craig asked.

"Just over a year."

"What did you think of him?"

Judith eyed him so coolly Craig thought she was going to ask him what business that was of his, but instead she answered, "He was more professional in his work than anybody I've ever known."

"But you didn't like him."

"Not very much, no. He was too calculating. He could be charming, but you always felt there was a reason for everything he did. As if he'd worked it all out in advance, what he'd say and how people would react."

"He was planning something for this weekend," Craig said. "Do you know what it was?"

Judith, watching the fingers of her left hand toying with a fork, didn't answer at once, and Craig guessed she was considering how much to tell him. He was aware for the first time of the different noises around them, the conversation of the other customers, the occasional shouts in the kitchen and the rattle of crockery. It was very warm and there was a faint odour of cooking.

"What do you mean, planning something?" Judith asked.

"On Saturday morning he admitted that he was up to something and said that we'd all know what it was yesterday," Craig told her. "It was a sort of game, he said. I don't think it was. I think it was deadly serious—and dangerous."

The waiter returned with the melon they had

both ordered, asked if they wanted pepper and, when Craig said yes, wielded a long wooden pepper mill with great aplomb.

"Why do you want to know?" Judith asked when he had gone. "What difference does it make now? He's dead."

"Because it's why he was killed. There's another reason: he asked me there and I want to know why. We hadn't seen each other for nearly twenty years. I think he knew that what he was planning to do might turn out to be dangerous, and he wanted me there to keep an eye on things. But I couldn't do anything because he wouldn't tell me what he was up to."

"I don't know," Judith said uncertainly.

"It'll come out sooner or later."

"I suppose so."

"It was something to do with the Randall case, wasn't it?"

"What makes you say that?"

Craig told her about the copy of the newspaper report Jordan had sent him, and how Micky had invited three of the Randalls' guests for the weekend.

"I'm not sure," she said, a frown puckering the creamy skin of her forehead. "He had pencilled in the case as a possible idea for one of his programmes, and we'd done some research for it."

Craig felt his senses quicken with anticipation. "What did you find out?" he asked.

"Not a lot. We traced the people who were staying at the house when Nigel Randall was shot. It wasn't called the White House then, it was Bensons. At least, we traced most of them; three were dead."

"What about the Fenns?" Craig asked.

"They live in Spain. Mrs. Fenn is an invalid and they couldn't travel."

So that was why Micky had had to settle for their son, Craig thought. He could hardly insist they come if they refused.

"You knew Micky had bought the Randalls' old house then?" he said.

"Yes. I went down there twice when we were working on the last series, and he told me about it. It's a lovely house." Judith paused. "Why do you call him Micky?"

"It's what we called him at school. His real name was Michael. You know why he wanted the Randalls' guests there?"

"No." Judith shook her head and her earrings danced.

"He was going to reconstruct what happened thirty years ago. You're sure he didn't say anything about it to you?"

"No. He never said much about his ideas until he had everything worked out. I did think he seemed very pleased with that one though. I assumed he'd got some theory about who really killed Randall and he was going to film interviews with the people who were there. I didn't know he'd invited them for this weekend. I'm afraid I didn't take very much notice, people are always having ideas about who really committed old murders, aren't they? Look at Jack the Ripper and that girl who killed her brother."

"Constance Kent," Craig said. "Could he have arranged for a camera crew to go down to the house?"

"I suppose he could." Judith looked startled. "But why should he?"

"To film a trial," Craig told her. "He believed he knew who really murdered Randall and kept quiet when Susan was sentenced to death for it. If I'm right, he meant to accuse them yesterday in front of the rest of us and film the scene for his programme."

Judith looked distressed. "That's rather horrible," she said.

"Yes," Craig agreed. "But is it something he was capable of doing?"

"He might. If he cared enough."

"He cared all right. The whole business had become an obsession with him." Craig paused. "Could you find out if he had laid on anything with a crew?"

"Yes, all right," Judith said. "I thought he was pleased with himself because he'd found a new angle for a programme. He was always saying we had to find new ways of looking at things. It wouldn't have mattered much if it was what really happened all those years ago or not, so long as it made good television."

"It mattered this time," Craig told her.

"Why so specially?"

"Because he couldn't face the possibility that Susan Randall had murdered her husband. She was his mother."

"*Miles?*" Judith gaped at him.

Craig nodded. "His real name was Michael Randall."

Jordan's office was large and more appropriate for a tycoon in business than a television presenter, Craig thought. But then, Jordan had been on his way to becoming a tycoon; there were four companies he owned with offices on this floor.

"Where did he keep the information he collected for his programmes?" he asked.

"In those files over there." Judith nodded towards two rather elegant cabinets against a wall and Craig walked over to them. "I don't think I should let you see them. Some of the things in there are very confidential."

"Jordan's been murdered," Craig said. "His notes may be important."

He waited while Judith hesitated a little longer. "They're in the second drawer in the right-hand cabinet," she told him.

The file was labelled "PROGRAMME 6—The Nigel Randall Case" and contained a considerable sheaf of papers. Craig took them over to the desk, sat down, and started to read them.

The first part consisted of notes on the people involved in the old case and the other guests at the Randalls' party. None of the people was named, each being called by a single letter. They were not the initial letters of either their

Christian or their surnames, but Craig had no difficulty in identifying them.

It was soon apparent that Jordan had reached the same conclusion as to the identity of Randall's murderer as he had.

The second part of the file comprised a rough outline of the programme Jordan had intended making. It left no doubt he had planned some sort of trial. You fool, Micky, Craig thought. That was one weakness of people who spent so much of their time manipulating others, it didn't occur to them their puppets were flesh and blood and might strike back.

Judith was busy at the telephone. Craig heard her say, "Thanks, Ben. 'Bye," and saw her replace the phone.

"Miles arranged for a film crew to go down to the White House yesterday afternoon," she told him. "When I rang the studio after Sandra told me what had happened they cancelled it."

"Thank you," Craig said. He picked up some of the papers from the file. "I know it's asking a lot, but would it be possible for me to have copies of some of these notes for the police?"

Judith hesitated. "How do I know I can trust you? You might use them for something else."

"You don't."

"You could be planning to blackmail somebody."

"Hardly, there aren't any names." Craig did his best to look appealing. "Scout's honour."

"Were you a scout?"

"To be honest, no."

Judith laughed. "All right, I don't suppose it matters. But please, promise only to the police."

"Promise," Craig said.

Judith took the sheets and went away to copy them. In less than five minutes she was back.

"You're a doll," Craig told her. "That's worth dinner some time."

"Give me a call," Judith said.

Max Dooley was depressed. He felt like that more often nowadays and sometimes it worried him that depression might be a symptom of middle-age approaching. Usually for a while in the middle of the day with the aid of two or three whiskies and congenial company he was able to forget the less pleasant facts of life, but today he had lunched with a young and very bright recruit to the paper's editorial staff and now he was more depressed than ever.

Craig's question did nothing to lighten his

gloom. He wondered what mess the young clot had got himself into this time. Stories of MPs' lack of integrity were nothing new and usually unfounded. They were also dangerous. Dooley was experienced enough to want something more than rumour to persuade him to take an active interest in yet another of them. At the same time, he had been in the game too long to be surprised or shocked, although Laxton's wasn't one of the first names he would have expected to be mentioned in that sort of context.

"You're telling me you think he's involved in something crooked?" he asked, gently probing his right ear with the tip of his letter opener.

"I didn't say crooked," Craig pointed out. "Just something he doesn't want anybody to know about."

"Sex?" Dooley suggested. "It usually is."

"I reckon not."

"And you want to know what it is?"

Craig nodded.

Dooley withdrew the letter opener, surveyed the point, to which a minute particle of wax was adhering, and wiped it with his handkerchief. "Why do you want to know?" he enquired. "Are you thinking of going in for a spot of blackmail on the side?"

"I'm working on a murder case," Craig told him, ignoring the irony.

For the first time that afternoon the journalist's professional interest was aroused. "Murder?" he repeated.

Craig grinned. "Later," he said.

Dooley wasn't an unkind man, and he was generally ready to help other people provided doing so required no more than the minimum of effort. Besides, murder was one of the headline subjects which appealed to a journalist's soul.

"Okay," he said. "I'll see if I can dig out anything."

"Thanks."

"My pleasure." Dooley felt a self-righteous glow and his depression lifted a little. He wasn't a bad sort, he had gone out of his way to help a fellow man down on his luck.

Craig said goodbye, walked across the landing to the lift, and pressed the button for the ground floor. Outside it had started to rain, large widely spaced thunder spots. Girls in thin summer dresses hurried by, hoping to reach wherever they were going before it came down in earnest, their heels tapping the pavement impatiently. Craig walked back to his office.

"Tea?" Georgie called as he passed.

"Thanks," he said.

There were no messages on his answering machine, and sitting down at his desk he began studying the notes he had made that morning.

"D'you know 'oo did it then?" Georgie enquired, coming in with his tea a few minutes later.

"That depends on what you mean by 'it'," Craig replied. "I'm waiting for a phone call; when it comes I'll have to go back to Lower Marking."

"You're never 'ere these days."

"Do you miss me, Georgie?"

"Like I miss a cold in the 'ead."

Craig sighed. "A policeman's lot is not a happy one."

"And you're not a p'liceman. Not any longer."

"It's worse for a private detective."

Georgie departed with a snort and Craig returned to his notes.

It was a long time before his call came. By then Georgie had gone home and the cleaners were loose on the top floors of the building, shuffling from room to room to the accompanying moan of electric cleaners. When the phone rang, although he had been expecting it, Craig started.

It was Dooley. One of the paper's lobby correspondents had heard a rumour that for years Laxton had been on the payroll of a property company which had recently acquired considerable well deserved notoriety. There had been hints of corruption in the Press, and more open allegations in Parliament. The correspondent had been unable to dig up any evidence to substantiate the rumours, and in the end he had written them off as just one more story which might be true but couldn't be proved. Or used.

Craig thanked Dooley and replaced the phone. If the story was true, and it became public knowledge, it would mean the end of Laxton's career. It was unlikely his constituency executive would look kindly on his accepting payments from the company, however innocently.

Craig went back to his notes, taking every fact and checking it meticulously. Examining again every suspect's motive and opportunity for committing both murders. Two questions in particular had bothered him for some time: how had the murderer known Jordan would be in the summerhouse on Saturday afternoon long enough in advance to plan the crime, and how had he carried the gun there undetected? He already knew the answer to the second and when, twenty minutes later, he pushed the notes aside and stretched, he believed he knew the other. It had been locked in his own memory. He knew now who had killed Micky Jordan and Gabriella, and how it had been done, but he felt no triumph. Not even satisfaction.

Walking across to the window, he looked out. Craig liked this time of the day in the City, when there was almost no traffic and hardly any pedestrians, when the streets were quiet and evening brought a few hours' respite from the noise and bustle of the day.

After a minute or two he turned, picked up the phone again, and dialled Granger's divisional headquarters. The Superintendent was still there and they talked briefly. Then, stuffing his notes into his pocket, Craig locked up and walked round the corner to where he had parked his car hours before. A ticket was tucked under one of the wiper blades.

Granger was in his office, a bleak, shabby room with a view of a yard and furniture which looked as if it had been picked up cheap at a second-hand dealer's a long time ago. His face was drawn with fatigue.

"You said you wanted to see me, so I waited," he greeted the younger man. "What's it about?"

"I thought you'd like a progress report," Craig told him.

Granger eyed him sourly. The sandwiches he had eaten too fast a couple of hours ago were sitting heavy in his stomach and he thought resentfully that if it hadn't been for Craig he would have been home by now, eating a proper meal with his wife and Debbie.

"I can do without the humour," he growled. "You mean progress?"

"I reckon so." Craig paused. "I think I know who killed Nigel Randall."

Granger didn't look excited. "So do I. Susan Randall."

"No. If she was guilty, why did Jordan stage his pantomime? He may have been keen to show she didn't do it—after all, she was his mother—but he wouldn't have wanted it all raked up again, and he wouldn't have gone to the lengths he did if he hadn't unearthed something pretty conclusive. I've talked to his PA. Did you know he'd arranged for a camera crew to film what he was planning to put on yesterday afternoon?"

"And what was that?" Granger demanded, interested in spite of himself.

"A new trial."

"*What?*"

"That's right. He had a defendant, he was going to be prosecutor and judge, and the viewers the jury. Only they wouldn't have any choice, there'd be only one possible verdict." Craig passed three pages of the notes Judith Cromer had copied across the desk. "They were in a file at his office, it's all there."

Granger glanced at the first page. "He'd never have got away with it," he protested.

"He might have done. It's not going that much further than some programmes have before. And he got away with most things."

Granger read the other two pages. "He must have been round the twist," he commented. "There aren't any names here, who did he think killed Randall?"

"Rupert Bateman."

For a second or two the Superintendent

didn't speak. Then he said in a tone of quiet reasonableness, "He can't have done, he was with his wife. She wouldn't have perjured herself to protect him, their marriage was breaking up and she was having it off with Randall."

"That's what she says. It's true, too—and it seemed good enough at the time. What nobody knew then was that Bateman was going to let her divorce him although she was the 'guilty' one."

"That often happened."

"I know. But not many husbands in Bateman's position made over nearly everything they had so that their unfaithful wives could live in comfort. He did, and it nearly bankrupted him. But nobody's suggested he was an angel—or that sort of fool."

"You're saying he did it to pay for an alibi?" Granger's tone was heavy with disbelief.

"Yes," Craig told him. "Look, there were the Randalls themselves and eight guests at the house that weekend. You can eliminate the four who were playing tennis when Randall was shot. That leaves Susan, Lorraine Maxwell, Laxton and the Batemans. Lorraine and Laxton were having a tumble in the house: Tom Levine says a maid went into the room for something, saw them, and slipped out again without their noticing her. If we accept Susan Randall didn't kill her husband, it has to be one or both of the Batemans. I don't know about you, but Caroline doesn't strike me as the sort to go for a walk by the river alone, and I doubt if she was then. I reckon she went to the summerhouse to have it out with Randall. He was after Lorraine and Caroline was on the way out. She wouldn't take that without making a scene.

"Bateman guessed where she'd gone. When he and his partner finished their set he left the others to carry on, fetched the gun he'd brought with him, and went after her. When he saw Caroline coming away from the summerhouse he went there, Randall probably laughed at him, and he shot him, dropping his gun and hurrying back towards the house. Caroline was lying when she said she met him coming from the tennis court, Laxton told me he'd wandered off some time before. He told her what he'd done and begged her to give him an alibi. Caroline must have been mad with Randall and maybe she was still fond of Bateman. Anyway, she'd do almost anything for money, and she agreed on condition he let her divorce him and gave her most of everything he had. He hadn't much choice—or thought he hadn't; he didn't see that he was her alibi as much as she was his.

"Then Susan Randall came along. It counted against her at the trial that she was wearing gloves, the prosecution claimed it showed she'd planned the murder before. But in those days women wore gloves to go out."

"You're saying she really went to tell Randall she was going somewhere and leaving their guests?" Granger asked doubtfully.

"Yes. She was in love with another man. His mother rang that afternoon to tell her he'd been knocked down and taken to hospital."

"How do you know all this?"

"Lorraine Maxwell told me."

Granger swore. "Why didn't she say anything to me?"

"You didn't ask her."

"All right then, why didn't it come out at the trial?"

"The boy friend died just before it started and probably she didn't want his family dragged into it. Or her counsel advised her not to mention it because it gave her a stronger motive for shooting her husband."

The Superintendent looked shaken.

"She asked the Batemans if they'd seen him. Caroline said she thought she'd heard somebody in the summerhouse and Susan hurried on. When she screamed they ran back and found her standing looking down at Randall stretched out on the floor and the gun at his feet, just as they said they did at the trial. But if you read the reports, you'll see she claimed she'd heard a noise that could have been the shot before she met the Batemans. They swore it was after and nobody believed her."

Granger was staring at the top of his desk as if he had never seen its scratched and worn surface before. Craig waited for him to say something, and when he didn't he went on, "You have to admit Bateman was a far likelier murderer than Susan. He was an ex-officer so he had almost certainly been trained to use a revolver—she was more likely to shoot off her own foot or put the bullet through the roof— and everybody says he was a weak, unstable character who was in love with his wife and knew she was having an affair with Randall. If Caroline wasn't blackmailing him, why was he so generous when they were divorced? Apparently he went to pieces after the trial and started drinking like a fish. That's not surprising if he had Mrs. Randall on his conscience—apart from the murder."

There was a lengthy silence. A car drove into the yard and pulled up. Doors slammed and a man called something Craig didn't catch, to be answered by a laugh from another. Footsteps sounded just outside the window, then stopped as the two men entered the building.

"I suppose it's possible," Granger conceded at last.

Craig grinned. "You don't give up easily, do you?"

The older man ignored the jibe. "Are you saying Caroline Rogers shot Jordan because he was going to accuse her of shooting Randall in one of his programmes?"

"No. Nobody could have proved anything after all this time, and the evidence is all circumstantial. Besides, the television company might let him make the programme, but when it came to the point I doubt if they'd dare show it."

"Jordan would have known that."

"He was so obsessed with the idea he probably didn't see the obstacles. And they might have shown it. Just. But if Caroline killed him and Gabriella, it wasn't because of what she was afraid he'd do."

"If you're right," Granger said slowly, "and Bateman killed Randall and she was an accessory, who else had a motive for killing Jordan?"

"Several people," Craig answered. "Because his murder had nothing to do with what happened in 1954."

Granger stared at him. "Are you telling me—" he began.

Craig interrupted him. "At least, there was no direct connection. What's the thing that struck you most about this weekend's party?"

"What I said before, that it was too damned stagey."

"That's right, the whole set-up was too theatrical. Even the casting. Apart from Gail Lakeland and me, all the guests were either there when Randall was shot or at least one of their close relatives was. So why were the two of us invited?"

"Miss Lakeland was his latest girl friend. You were supposed to protect him." Granger permitted himself a hint of malice.

"That's how it looked. But think who was there in 1954: Lorraine Maxwell, the Batemans,

Laxton, Peter Fenn, Jane Marsh, Phillipson and Mary Whittaker. Caroline, Lorraine and Laxton were there this weekend. Bateman was dead. Jane Marsh married Fenn; they live in Spain and couldn't come, so Micky invited their son and his wife. Phillipson died without marrying. That leaves Mary Whittaker."

"She's dead," Granger said. "She couldn't be there."

"I know," Craig agreed. "She committed suicide in 1970. I spent part of this afternoon at St. Catherine's House looking up the old registers of births and marriages, and talking to a man I know. Mary Whittaker was the daughter of Lord Somebody-or-other, Whittaker was her stage name. She wasn't much good as an actress—or as a wife either. She married a doctor, but she left him and shacked up with a petty crook named Rawlings. By that time she was on drugs and she was done for soliciting and robbery, amongst other things. She left Rawlings, or he left her, and in 1970 she shot the man she was living with then and pumped herself full of heroin. It made quite a feast for the papers."

"It would," Granger agreed bitterly. "You say her husband was a doctor?"

Craig nodded. "He's still alive; he practises not far from here. His name's George Lakeland."

15

"GAIL LAKELAND!" Granger's expression betrayed his astonishment. "You think Jordan knew?"

"Oh, he knew all right," Craig said. "He had his research team trace everybody who stayed at the Randalls' that weekend. His PA knew all about Mary Whittaker. He got to know Gail deliberately, just like he did the others: he suggested to the publishers she works for that one of their authors might be on his programme. She made the arrangements. When she got here and realized what he was up to, she guessed he'd found out about her mother."

"She wouldn't want all that dragged up again," Granger commented. "It gives her a pretty strong motive."

"She may think her mother killed Randall and let Susan be convicted," Craig agreed. "She doesn't know about Bateman, and Mary Whittaker shot another man afterwards. There's another thing, she saw how Micky had used her. She's a proud girl, she can't have liked that."

"It all fits."

"Yes." Craig settled himself more comfortably. The chair was hard and what padding it possessed had long ago congealed into lumps. "Don't forget the second murder. Gabriella Fenn."

"She knew too much about the first one," Granger said.

"Yes. But what?"

"You tell me."

"I don't know for sure," Craig admitted, "but I can guess. After Fenn left her by the pool she got fed up and decided to go to see Jordan. Maybe she wanted to have it out with him because he'd dropped her for Gail Lakeland. The most direct way from that side of the pool to the summerhouse is by the path that runs along the side of the wood by the cornfield. Right?"

"I suppose so."

"If she met somebody, they were coming from the direction of the river. The murderer had just thrown Willy Davies' rifle into it, and that path was his—or her—best way of getting back again without being seen. For their meeting to mean anything to Gabriella it had to be someone she wouldn't have expected to be there at that time. Someone who claimed to be somewhere else."

"Gail Lakeland," Granger said.

"It could have been almost any of them." Craig was reflecting that when she left him Gail had made for the wood. Could she have retrieved the gun from some hiding place where she had concealed it earlier, shot Jordan, thrown the gun in the river, and been returning to the house when Gabriella came along? Not if the shots had been fired while the two planes were flying over, she had been playing tennis with him then.

Gail wasn't the only one to consider, there were Fenn (whom, a short time before, he had seen walking towards the old stables), one or both of the Laxtons, even Lorraine. And Caroline. True, he had seen the MP and his wife admiring the roses as he went towards the house, but there would have been plenty of time for one of them to hurry down to the summerhouse, shoot Micky, and rejoin the other while he and Gail were finishing their second set and his back was to them much of the time. He hadn't been paying much attention to them, anyway.

When they finished playing Lorraine had disappeared. She claimed she had gone to talk to Jordan and found him dead, but was that part of it true?

Craig thought that hardly anybody used the path by the cornfield, but because of her infatuation with Jordan Gabriella had done so on Saturday, and it had cost her her life. He had considered them all there in his office while other workers went home and in the street outside the traffic thinned. Now he was satisfied that he knew what Gabriella had seen, but could he convince Granger?

"Did you find anything in Jordan's wardrobe?" he enquired.

The Superintendent nodded. "They were still there. The forensic people are looking at them now, but I don't think there's much doubt." Craig didn't either. "Do you want to hear what I think happened?" he asked.

In a sharper voice, Granger said, "You know?"

"I think so. If I tell you my idea you can pick holes in it. Okay?"

It didn't take long. When Craig had finished

Granger said nothing for nearly twenty seconds, then he observed grimly, "It fits. And that was who Miss Maxwell saw in the trees?"

"I reckon so."

"It's going to be hard proving it."

"Yes." Craig eased his aching muscles. He remembered that he hadn't eaten since lunch and it was now nearly ten. "What will you do?"

"The usual things. We'd better get up there as quickly as possible."

"Has anyone else left?"

"Not since the Laxtons."

"Willy Davies is still there?"

"He'd better be." Granger eyed Craig levelly. "You may as well come along."

Craig hesitated. Why did the CID man want him there? It wasn't his case, all he had done was suggest what he believed had happened. He would much rather not be involved in what happened from now on. On the other hand, to refuse to go might seem like turning his back on what he had brought about. He wished profoundly Granger hadn't suggested he should.

"All right," he agreed.

It was nearly dark when the three cars, with Craig's Dolomite bringing up the rear, turned off the road between the massed shadows of the rhododendrons. The Press men had gone, satisfied that there was nothing to be gained from a long boring vigil and that any new developments would be reported to them at tomorrow's Press conference. Ahead the house looked pale and insubstantial in the dusk. Lights showed in two of the ground floor windows, but the rest was in darkness.

As the leading car rounded the gentle curve of the drive its headlights lit up the rosebuds and the lawns, then the house itself, bringing it to life. There was a light in the police caravan, but to the right the old stable block was dark. Craig wondered where the Davieses were. Then the driver of the first car stopped with a gentle crunch of gravel, the others pulled up behind it, and men got out.

"Matthews, Rider, Benson . . ." Granger disposed his forces with the assurance of many years' experience. He knew what he had to do now, and he worked coolly and efficiently.

When he was satisfied his men had had time to reach their positions he stepped on to the verandah and rang the doorbell. There was no answer and he glanced at Craig. But if he expected to see anything in the younger man's expression he was disappointed, Craig's face was as inscrutable as his own. Behind them one of the men shuffled his feet, the slight sound seeming to be magnified tenfold by the previous silence.

Granger rang again. Craig felt his nerves tighten. Why didn't somebody come?

Then the door was opened and Gail stood there, her slim figure silhouetted against the light in the hall. To Craig it seemed there was something defensive in the way she was holding the door open only a few inches.

"Oh," she said. He caught the hint of dismay in her voice. "It's you, Superintendent."

"We'd like to come in, Miss Lakeland, please," Granger told her formally.

Gail glanced back over her shoulder, perhaps looking for Sandra to obtain her agreement. But there was nobody there and she stepped back, watching the men file into the hall with Craig bringing up the rear.

"Alan!" she exclaimed, seeing him for the first time. "You said you weren't—"

"I asked Mr. Craig to come along, Miss Lakeland," Granger told her.

"Oh." Gail hesitated. "You'd better come into the drawing-room."

Everything looked so normal, Craig thought. Lorraine Maxwell was sitting in an easy chair playing patience at a low table. As they walked in and she saw Granger her slender hands with their long scarlet-painted nails stopped turning over the cards and her eyes became watchful behind their barriers of mascaraed lashes. Fenn, in another chair, reading, looked up too. Gail walked across to the window recess and stood there, and again Craig had the impression she was on guard.

"Where are the others?" Granger asked.

Nobody answered at once and it was Fenn who countered, "Are you here to arrest somebody?"

This time it was the Superintendent who took no notice.

"I don't know where they are," Lorraine said. "Do you, honey?"

"I think Caroline's in her room," Gail replied. "Sandra's probably in the kitchen."

"Where are the Davieses?" Craig enquired. "There's no light in their flat."

"I don't know."

"You think one of them . . . ?" Fenn began, sounding as if he couldn't believe it.

"Miss Lakeland," Granger said.

She faced him and Craig could see the alarm in her eyes.

The momentary silence was shattered by a woman's scream. It was stifled almost immediately, but not before it had torn at their nerves, already strung too tight. They all stared at the door. Craig heard Gail gasp and Granger curse quietly beside him.

Then the first seconds of shock passed and together they started out into the hall, Craig leading. The scream had come from the direction of the kitchen and he thrust open the door at the end of the hall. Beyond it the second door on the left was ajar. Flinging it wide, he charged in.

The kitchen was a large room with a good deal of clear space round the table in the middle. Sandra was pinned against the table, striving desperately to fend off Willy Davies who was attacking her frenziedly. He seemed deranged. His wife, distraught, was trying unsuccessfully to pull him away.

As Craig burst in the little Welshman put his hands round Sandra's throat. She twisted frantically, but she was helpless against the sinewy strength of the gardener. Craig leapt forward, shoved his right hand, straight armed, in

Davies's face and pushed. The Welshman staggered and his grip slackened. Craig gave him another violent shove that sent him floundering backwards to collide with a row of built in cupboards. Crockery rattled in one of them and a door came open.

Sandra straightened up. She was gasping for breath and Craig could see the marks of the gardener's thumbs on the pale skin of her throat. Apparently oblivious of Granger and the men who had followed him in from the hall, she clasped him as if to support herself.

"Oh, Alan," she gasped.

Craig was very conscious of the pressure of her body and the expression in her eyes. Gently he pushed her away. One of the policemen went across to where Davies was leaning, half collapsed, against the cupboards, all the fury drained out of him.

For a moment there was silence, then Granger stepped forward. "Mrs. Jordan," he said. "I have to tell you I'm not satisfied with the answers you have given to certain of the questions you have been asked concerning the deaths of your husband and Mrs. Fenn. I must ask you to come with me to the police station

278

to answer some further questions and make a new statement."

For perhaps five seconds Sandra stared at him, shocked. Then she turned viciously on Craig. "You!" she said, bitterly accusing. "This is your doing."

She thought she'd got away with it, Craig told himself. That's why she's so appalled now. He had seen the vanity, the hint of triumph in her eyes when she clung to him just now.

Granger nodded to his men and they took her out, a policeman on one side and a woman pc on the other. As if she were already under arrest, Craig thought. Two more men followed, Davies handcuffed to one of them. Seeing him now, crushed and looking smaller than ever between the burly policemen, it seemed an unnecessary precaution.

As Sandra and her escort emerged from the kitchen Caroline was coming down the stairs. She stopped, looking puzzled. Gail and Fenn stared, shocked, from the drawing room doorway, Lorraine just behind them.

"Sandra!" Gail breathed.

The older woman glanced at her, her pale features blank now, but she said nothing. A second or two later she was taken out to one of the waiting police cars and Davies to another.

"Are you coming?" Granger asked Craig.

"Not just yet." Craig looked at Gail. "Unless you'd rather I did."

"No," she said. "Stay, Alan. Please."

For a moment it seemed that the Superintendent was going to say something. If so, he changed his mind, for he started following the others out. In the doorway he turned. "I'll see you later?" he asked.

"Yes," Craig agreed.

They were in the drawing-room. Lorraine had moved the table out of the way and was sitting, as graceful as ever but showing signs of strain now, in her old chair, while Fenn was slumped in the one he had occupied before. Caroline, pale and unhealthy looking under her make-up, had taken one end of a settee. Gail was perched on another, and after a moment's hesitation while he told himself he couldn't keep standing as if he were lecturing them, Craig sat down beside her. A woman pc was with Joan Davies in the flat over the garages.

"That was kind of a shock," Lorraine

observed quietly. "It was to me anyway. I just never thought . . ."

"She hasn't been arrested yet," Craig pointed out.

"But she will be?"

"I think so. There isn't any doubt this time."

"What happened out there?" Fenn wanted to know. "Why did she scream?"

"Willy attacked her," Craig told him. "He thought the world of Micky because Micky stood up for him and gave him a job when he was having a bad time. But he couldn't stand Sandra. He'd got it into his head she wasn't good enough for Jordan. Maybe he saw something nobody else did. Then she more or less left Micky for another man, and that settled it as far as he was concerned. He probably hadn't worked out how she killed Jordan, but he'd made up his mind she did, and this evening it all boiled over. Perhaps she said something. Anyway, he nearly strangled her."

"Poor Willy," Gail said quietly. "What will happen to him?"

"I don't know. He'll be safer with the police than here for the time being; after that it'll depend on the quacks, I expect."

"I thought Sandra was talking to Joan when

Miles was shot—and it was all something to do with that man Randall having been murdered. But it can't have been, can it?"

Caroline had looked increasingly on edge, now she burst out, "Do we have to have an inquest? It's all over, can't we forget it now?"

Craig regarded her without sympathy. If you went back far enough, he thought, she was responsible for all that had happened these last three days; it was because of her greed all those years ago that two people were dead. He wondered if she understood that and was troubled by the knowledge. It seemed doubtful.

"Don't delude yourself it's over yet," he told her brutally.

Their eyes met and it was Caroline who looked away first. She's frightened, he told himself. She can't be sure that it won't all come out at the trial and that she won't still be charged. He turned back to Gail.

"Micky was the Randalls' son. It was his mother who was convicted of shooting his father in the summerhouse thirty years ago." From the gasps of surprise and startled expressions of the others Craig knew Lorraine hadn't told them. "He was only five and an uncle and aunt adopted him. He took their name, and he didn't

282

know himself who he really was until after his uncle died last year. I suppose he had idolised the mother he could hardly remember, and even when he was grown up he couldn't face the possibility that she had been a murderess. It became an obsession with him to show the world she hadn't been—and who had really killed his father and let his mother go to gaol for him. He bought this house, had his team of researchers trace everybody who was staying here that weekend, and worked out who the murderer must have been."

"It was Susan." Caroline had been staring at Craig as if there was something preventing her taking her eyes off him, and now when she spoke her voice was pitched too high.

"No," Craig told her. "Micky was right. There's evidence now the police didn't have at the time, and if you start by assuming she was innocent it isn't difficult to see who really shot Randall. I know who it was. So does Granger."

He paused and glanced across at Lorraine, but the actress's expression told him nothing. "He decided to make a television programme about the case, to broadcast the truth on one of the most popular shows on the air so that as many people as possible would see it," he went on. "Three of the Randalls' guests were dead, Roger Phillipson, Rupert Bateman and an actress called Mary Whittaker"—Craig could almost feel Gail, sitting only a foot away from him, tense, and he went on,—"but Bateman's widow was still alive. She'd remarried. Two of the others had married, too, but they lived in Spain and couldn't travel, so he invited their son and his wife in their place. He was going to New York on business anyway, and he fixed it so that he met Lorraine there, and when she told him she was coming over to Britain, he sent her an invitation."

"He rang me, too, to make sure I was coming," the actress said.

"He went to extraordinary lengths to get all the people he wanted together for his programme," Craig agreed.

"But why did he want us all here?" Fenn demanded. "He could have made it without us."

"A programme yes—but not a trial," Craig told him. "And that's what he planned. A public trial of the person whose perjury resulted in his mother's being sentenced to death and dying in prison so that he never saw her again. You heard him that first evening we were here,

284

you can see what an obsession it had become with him." Craig could tell that, for one or two of them at least, the idea was not only horrible but new as well. "He said he was staging a sort of game, and that's what it was to him, a terrible game with him stalking the person who had done that to him. He told you *you* had nothing to worry about, Simon. Which meant somebody else had."

Craig paused. "Granger's problem was that right from the start there were two possibilities: that Jordan was shot because of what he knew about Randall's murder and because it looked as if he was going to make that public, and two, that there was no connection between the two crimes, and he was shot for some quite different reason. Without knowing it, Micky had made things about as complicated as he could."

Briefly, and without mentioning Caroline's part in the events of thirty years before, Craig explained how he and Granger had finally decided that, despite all the evidence to the contrary, the murders weren't linked. "At least, not directly," he corrected himself. "Because Sandra knew roughly what Micky was up to and she used it."

"She knew?" Gail echoed.

285

"Yes. They may have more or less separated, but she said herself they were still on good terms. He couldn't tell anybody else what he was going to do, but it must have become so important to him by then that he had to share it with someone. So he told her. After all, it wasn't exactly illegal. She already knew how interested he was in the Randall business, he'd bought this house and talked to her about the murder months before they split up, and she wasn't involved. The only one of you she'd met was Caroline.

"When she wasn't here, Sandra lived with a man called Newton who runs a little pottery in the village. He's several years younger than her, and they say he's in trouble financially. Sandra hadn't any money of her own, and her parents weren't well off by any means. Not that Micky was as rich as you may think; his parents lived pretty extravagantly, this house was mortgaged to the hilt and they didn't leave him very much. His uncle and aunt weren't wealthy people either, and although he must have made a tidy bit from his work lately, it's only the last two or three years he's been a really big name. And he lived well. A large part of his capital was tied up in this house; he bought it with his legacies from his father and his uncle plus a hefty mortgage. The flat in London's rented."

"How do you know all this?" Gail asked.

"Part of it I found out myself after somebody here asked me to make some inquiries, part of it Granger told me this evening. He's talked to Micky's solicitor." Craig saw the girl's expression and added, "It was true what I said, I haven't any connection with the police. But when I learnt certain things I had to pass them on. It wasn't my idea I came back here this evening, Granger wanted me to."

"What difference does it make?" Fenn demanded.

"None," Craig agreed. He went on, "Sandra was ready to do almost anything for Newton. She must have reckoned that if she and Micky were divorced she would end up with a share of their joint property, and that wouldn't amount to much because he'd bought this house with his own money. She wanted enough to make a clean break, put Newton's business on its feet, and keep her in the style she'd grown used to. Micky hadn't made a will, and if he died she would inherit everything, including the house. I don't know whether she was right or not, and it doesn't matter, it's what she believed. She couldn't afford to wait because with their marriage breaking up fast he might make a will cutting her out at any time. When he told her about his party and what he was going to do she saw a way of achieving what she wanted. She rang him on Saturday morning and told him she must see him that afternoon."

"How do you know that?" Fenn asked.

"I was in the room with Jordan when she phoned. Only I didn't know who it was or what she was saying. All I heard was Micky say something like 'Must we?' and then 'Oh, all right then.' She must have asked him to meet her at the summerhouse, and to say nothing about it to anybody else. That would have sounded reasonable enough if she wanted to talk to him about their personal affairs."

"But she was with Joan Davies when Miles was killed," Gail protested.

"So she led us to believe. But we don't know exactly when the shot was fired, nobody heard it. Yet we all heard Caroline scream. That's why I think it was almost certainly while those planes were flying over. Their coming was sheer luck from her point of view, and afterwards she traded on it. But they'd gone before she arrived at the house and spoke to Mrs. Davies. Mrs.

Davies told me so. Later there was nothing to point to her any more than the rest of us—less, she wasn't one of the party and she had nothing to do with the Randall case.

"Look at it another way. None of us staying here knew Jordan was going to work in the summerhouse until he told us so after lunch, so we couldn't have planned the murder before then. A rifle, even a ·22 like Willy's, is a pretty conspicuous thing to carry around—especially when it's hot and people aren't wearing coats. Anyone who went to the stables, took it, and carried it down to the summerhouse while people were wandering about the gardens would have been running a tremendous risk. Even if they knew where Willy kept it. That bothered me, it seemed to point to the Davieses or somebody from outside. Then I saw that it could have been Sandra on the phone that morning, and that she could have come up from the village while we were having lunch and the Davieses were in the kitchen, stolen the gun, and taken it back to the village in her car.

"Newton's next-door neighbour had an old rowing boat he kept moored at the bottom of his garden. On Saturday afternoon she untied it and paddled upstream. The river's hardly overlooked at all along that stretch, so it wasn't likely anyone would see her until she was clear of the village, and after that the road's some way off. It's not very far to the summerhouse, and there's very little traffic on the road, but Granger did find a man who said he'd seen a girl in a boat some distance away as he was driving across the bridge. She paddled right up to the summerhouse, shot Jordan twice, and took the sheet of paper from his typewriter to make it look as if he'd been killed to prevent something he knew being made public. Then she pushed the boat out into mid-stream so that it drifted down until it got caught up in the bank, walked on a little way, threw the rifle into the river, and hurried up to the house by the path along the side of the cornfield. All that wouldn't have taken her more than three minutes. She found Mrs. Davies in the kitchen, and within four minutes of shooting Micky she was asking where he was."

"It's horrible," Gail said quietly.

"I guess it's being so calculated makes it seem worse," Lorraine agreed. "I liked Sandra."

"Yes." Craig paused. "She said she spoke to Joan Davies, and both Granger and I assumed she'd come into the house. Then last night Mrs.

Davies said she'd come up to the window. When I thought about it that struck me as odd —unless she had approached the house from the back through the copse. She didn't want anybody to see her because she'd come from the river not the village. Unfortunately Gabriella had seen her on the path and let Sandra know she had. So Sandra had to kill her too. Yesterday afternoon she drew the curtains on the side of the house overlooking the pool— everybody assumed it was because of the sun; it seemed reasonable—and bolted the French windows so that nobody was likely to go out that way and see her. She wore dark trousers and a jacket and hat of Micky's. The hat was a giveaway, how many men wear hats in the country on hot summer days? But she had to wear it to hide her hair and shade her face."

"I only caught a glimpse of her through the trees," Lorraine said, "but I thought it was a man."

Craig glanced at Fenn. "I'm sorry, Simon, but I found the jacket in Micky's wardrobe with a smear of make-up on one cuff where Sandra put her hand over Gabriella's mouth. It's not as easy as people sometimes think to kill a person by stabbing them once. That suggested whoever killed Gabriella was either lucky, for want of a better word, or had medical knowledge. And they had strong nerves, too, to do it with people only thirty yards away. Sandra was a nurse before she and Micky were married, and apart from a knowledge of anatomy nurses have to learn to keep cool in emergencies. She was the only one who knew Micky would be in the summerhouse in time to plan the murder and the only one who definitely knew where Willy kept his gun. There were other things, too, little things in themselves, but when you can see the whole picture they become significant. Like the way she told me Willy had had rows with Micky, and that he frightened her. She was careful not to lay it on too thick."

Had she asked him to walk with her on Saturday evening in order to pump him? Craig wondered. Or perhaps to divert any suspicions he might have away from her? He wished he could remember everything she had said.

"You thought it might be me," Gail told him quietly.

"He had to consider everybody, honey," Lorraine said. Already, Craig noticed, she looked more calm and composed.

"But he had a special reason for suspecting

me." Gail was looking up at him. "Didn't you?"

His eyes met hers. "No," he replied. "I just wondered if it could have been Micky who wanted to break it off and not you, that's all. But if he was shot while those planes were going over you couldn't have done it, we were still playing tennis."

He could see she didn't believe him, and wondered if it mattered to her what he thought. After all, why should it?

"Gabriella knew something," Fenn observed.

"About Sandra. You misunderstood and thought she was talking about Gail." Craig paused. "I'd better go, Granger wants to see me."

They made no move to detain him any longer and he walked to the door, opened it and stepped out into the hall. Already they wanted to forget all that had happened, he told himself, and because he was part of it they wanted to forget him too.

Outside the air was pleasantly cool. He walked over to the Triumph, started the engine, and drove down the long drive to the road.

Other titles in the
Linford Mystery Library:

STORM CENTRE
by Douglas Clark
Detective Chief Superintendent Masters, temporarily lecturing in a police staff college, finds there's more to the job than a few weeks' relaxation in a rural setting. He soon gets involved in a local police problem.

THE MANUSCRIPT MURDERS
by Roy Harley Lewis
Antiquarian bookseller Matthew Coll, acquires a rare 16th century manuscript. But when the Dutch professor who had discovered the journal is murdered, Coll begins to doubt its authenticity.

SHARENDEL
by Margaret Carr
Ruth had loved Aunt Cass. She didn't want all that money. And she didn't want Aunt Cass to die. But at Sharendel things looked different. She began to wonder if she had a split personality.

MURDER TO BURN
by Laurie Mantell

Sergeants Steven Arrow and Lance Brendon, of the New Zealand police force, come upon a woman's body floating in the water. When the dead woman is finally identified the police begin to realise that they are investigating a fascinatingly complex fraud.

YOU CAN HELP ME
by Maisie Birmingham

Whilst running the Citizens' Advice Bureau, Kate Weatherley is attacked with no apparent motive. Then the body of one of her clients is found in her room.

DAGGERS DRAWN
by Margaret Carr

Stacey Manston was the kind of girl who could take most things in her stride, but three murders were something different – especially as she had the motive and opportunity to kill them all . . .

THE MONTMARTRE MURDERS
by Richard Grayson

Inspector Gautier of Sûreté investigates the disappearance of artist Théo, the heir to a fortune. Then a shady art dealer is murdered and the plot begins to focus on three paintings by a seemingly obscure artist.

GRIZZLY TRAIL
by Gwen Moffat

Miss Pink, alone in the Rockies, helps in a search for missing hikers, solves two cruel murders and has the most terrifying experience of her life when she meets a grizzly bear!

BLINDMAN'S BLUFF
by Margaret Carr

Kate Deverill had considered suicide. It was one way out—and preferable to being murdered. Better than waiting for the blow to strike, waiting and wondering . . .

BEGOTTEN MURDER
by Martin Carroll

When Susan Phillips joined her aunt on a voyage of 12,000 miles from her home in Melbourne, she little knew their arrival would germinate the seeds of murder planted long ago.

WHO'S THE TARGET?
by Margaret Carr

Three people whom Abby could identify as her parents' murderers wanted her dead, but she decided that maybe Jason could have been the target. Then Abby was attacked in the old ruins and she wondered if she could be wrong after all.

THE LOOSE SCREW
by Gerald Hammond

After a motor smash, Beau Pepys and his cousin Jacqueline, her fiancé and dotty mother, suspect that someone had pre-arranged the death of their friend. But who, and why, and above all, how?

SANCTUARY ISLE
by Bill Knox

Chief Detective Inspector Colin Thane and Detective Inspector Phil Moss are sent to a bird sanctuary off the coast of Argyll to investigate the murder of the warden.

THE SNOW ON THE BEN
by Ian Stuart

Although on holiday in the Highlands, Chief Inspector Hamish MacLeod begins an investigation when a pistol shot shatters the quiet of his solitary morning walk. And then one of his suspects is found drowned.

HARD CONTRACT
by Basil Copper

Private detective Mike Farraday is hired by Eli Dancer to obtain settlement of a debt from Minsky. But Minsky is killed before Mike can get to him. A spate of murders follows.

CASE WITH THREE HUSBANDS
by Margaret Erskine

Was it a ghost of one of Rose Bonner's late husbands that gave her old Aunt Agatha such a terrible shock and then murdered her in her bed? The Bonner family felt that only Inspector Septimus Finch could catch the killer.

THE END OF THE RUNNING
by Alan Evans

Lang continued to push the men and children on and on. Behind them were the men who were hunting them down, waiting for the first signs of exhaustion before they pounced.

CARNABY AND THE HIJACKERS
by Peter N. Walker

When Commander Pigeon assigns Detective Sergeant Carnaby-King to prevent a raid on a bullion-carrying passenger train, he knows that there are traitors in high positions within the railway, banking and even police circles.

TREAD WARILY AT MIDNIGHT
by Margaret Carr

If Joanna Morse hadn't been so hasty she wouldn't have been involved in the accident, and wouldn't have offered hospitality to the injured woman, only to find she was an escaped inmate from the local nursing home.

TOO BEAUTIFUL TO DIE
by Martin Carroll

There was a grave in the churchyard to prove Elizabeth Weston was dead. Alive, she presented a problem. Dead, she could be forgotten. Then, in the eighth year of her death she came back. She was beautiful, but she had to die.

IN COLD PURSUIT
by Ursula Curtiss

In Mexico, Mary and her cousin Jenny each encounter strange men, but neither of them realises that one of these men is obsessed with revenge and murder. But which one?

LITTLE DROPS OF BLOOD
by Bill Knox

It might have been just another unfortunate road accident but a few little drops of blood pointed to murder—and plunged Chief Inspector Colin Thane and Inspector Phil Moss into another adventure.

GOSSIP TO THE GRAVE
by Jonathan Burke

Jenny Clark invented Simon Sherborne because her daily gossip column was getting dull. But when the society editor demanded a picture of the elusive playboy, Jenny knew she had to get rid of him. Then Simon appeared at a party—in the flesh! And Jenny finds herself involved in murder.

HARRIET FAREWELL
by Margaret Erskine

Wealthy Theodore Buckler had planned a magnificent Guy Fawkes Day celebration. He hadn't planned on murder.